TWO GRAVES AT HELLSGATE

Jack Brown had thrown away seven years of his life hunting for ex-Sergeant Marvin Hasher, believing him to be the man behind his brother's death and an unsolved case of theft. When Brown finally caught up with him, Hasher told him what had really happened that night the Civil War had ended. Then Hasher was gunned down in circumstances that forced Brown to start thinking about the men around him. Soon it was all hell-for-leather!

Books by Jeff Blaine
in the Linford Western Library:

BLACK JO OF THE PECOS

JEFF BLAINE

TWO GRAVES AT HELLSGATE

Complete and Unabridged

LINFORD
Leicester

First published in Great Britain in 1997 by
Robert Hale Limited
London

First Linford Edition
published 1998
by arrangement with
Robert Hale Limited
London

British Library CIP Data

Blaine, Jeff, 1928–
    Two graves at Hellsgate.—Large print ed.—
Linford western library
    1. Western stories
    2. Large type books
    I. Title
    823.9'14 [F]

    ISBN 0–7089–5322–0

Published by
F. A. Thorpe (Publishing) Ltd.
Anstey, Leicestershire

Set by Words & Graphics Ltd.
Anstey, Leicestershire
Printed and bound in Great Britain by
T. J. International Ltd., Padstow, Cornwall

This book is printed on acid-free paper

1

This was it. Jack Brown was about to fulfil his grim dream of the last seven years. He was on the brink of killing Marvin Hasher. "Draw, you son-of-a-bitch!" he rasped, hatred clutching at his throat.

Hasher stood there opposite him — at the other end of Goodman's Long Bar indeed — and he still made a big target. Yet the ravages of hard years were upon him, and he was all eyes and jutting bones. It was obvious that he was far from well; but he wasn't scared for all that, and he was tensing to make his move.

But then he started to cough; and he coughed horribly, catching at his mouth with both hands, and a fine spray of blood and sputum flew out from between his fingers. The tension left him, and his upper body slumped forward weakly. Yet there was no loss of courage in his eyes, and his expression seemed only to plead for the chance to recover himself and make a fair fight of it.

For all his terrible hatred of the man, Brown held his draw. He looked hard and deep into the other's being, and what he saw there sobered him, for the voice at the bottom of his mind — seldom heard and unacknowledged before today — was again telling him that he could be wrong. It was quite possible that Hasher had been speaking the truth just now. When all was said and done, it had been as black as black hogs that fateful night, when the news had come into camp that the Civil War had ended and that they were all civilians again and once more responsible for their own lives and futures. There, with the fire burning low and red, greed had raised its ugly head once more and men had started thinking selfishly again. Beside the fire had stood those saddlebags containing that Yankee gold — pay for a regiment or two, and seized only that morning after a bitter cavalry action — and all eyes had come to rest upon it and voices had begun to question through the surrounding darkness in confused whispers.

Only heaven could tell what pressing evil had entered the more susceptible of the minds present — if it had indeed been the spur of the moment business which Jack Brown had always supposed it to be — but suddenly the gun-crazy ruthlessness which had for so long been reserved for actions with the enemy had erupted in the Confederate encampment and comrade had turned on comrade and that old-time lust for money and the things it could buy had replaced the selfless generosity of spirit which had given all to the Southern cause and never for a moment counted the cost.

Brown's memory filled with gun-flashes. Scarlet flame had seemed to dart at him from all directions. There had been hubbub all over the auction, and Brown had been fumbling rather ineffectually at his holster — trying to make up his mind whether there was any side to be on but his own — when he had spotted his brother Frank running to join him through the fireglow, and Frank had just drawn even with him when the poor devil had kicked back in his stride and buckled to the ground. Then, a split second later, a slug had clipped the crown of Brown's skull and flattened him too. And there he and Frank had lain side by side on soil which they had irrigated liberally with their blood during the long night that had followed.

But Jack Brown had recovered his senses with the dawn, while his brother Frank had gone on lying there, dead forever, and Jack, filled with grief and fury, had later buried him at that spot, muttering to himself promises of revenge on the men who had slain him and others in the process of robbing their own cavalry troop. But it hadn't been that easy for, when it was all over, a consternation had persisted which, even after some kind of discipline had been restored in camp, the inquiry instituted by Colonel Clyde Riches and Captain George Bayes had done little to resolve or clarify. It had been determined, though, that Sergeant Marvin Hasher, Corporal Abel Tyson, and Troopers Dibber, Forder and Lumley, were missing from the company and could only be accounted as the actual thieves. Riders had been despatched to pursue them but, between the military restrictions imposed on the soldiers by the fact of Lee's surrender and the all-pervading apathy of defeat in the Confederate ranks, the chase had spluttered out when confronted by Yankee patrols and the hunters had not even bothered to report back to their unit or provide any written account of their doings. Brown had probed into the matter immediately after the surrender period, but learned nothing beyond the facts that the Union gold had never been recovered and that Sergeant Hasher and his friends had made no effort anywhere to muster out and had seemed to have been swallowed by the land. There the basic mystery of what had actually occurred on that dark and chilly night in April 1865 remained to this day; with the difference that Brown had caught up with Hasher at long last, and now —

"Cough on, Marvin!" Brown advised, realizing that his tones contained more of contempt for the other's physical weakness than the reasonableness — which was one of the better parts of his nature — had intended. "Bring up your lungs, man! There's a cure for your trouble, and I've got it. Hot lead will put anything right. Do you recall Harry Spode? He had a cough just like yours. But that musket ball at the Junction sure saw to him!"

Hasher looked back hard, yet couldn't quite manage to glower, and his fit of coughing grew even worse and he stooped into semi-collapse over the green baize top of a card table, his braced arms supporting him and his hands spread.

Brown was shocked despite himself. He walked slowly up to the sick man. There he pulled out a chair and sat the other down, snapping his fingers towards the bar for quick service from the 'tender lingering there and demanding a bottle of rye and a glass. These were supplied by hands that seemed to reach abnormally long and far and, nodding, Brown took the bottle and glass and poured for his enemy, inwardly aghast that he was doing such a thing and even feeling a certain compassion as he did it. "Get this into you," he said gruffly, putting the drink to Hasher's lips and tipping.

Hasher swallowed a drop or two of the spirit, gasping, then took the glass from Brown's fingers and shot the rest of the drink down his gullet, sleeving off and muttering a word of thanks.

"Have another," Brown ordered, refilling the glass. "Get it back now! With luck, it'll choke you; and that'll save me shooting you."

"Gid out of it!" Hasher croaked. "Your heart's the size of — a chamber-pot!"

"Ain't it, though!" Brown agreed sourly, spitting accurately into a nearby spittoon. "You never were any damned good!"

"You should know, feller," Hasher commented, falling back in his chair weakly and shutting his eyes as the hundred proof rye began putting a little bit of colour back into his cheeks. "You and that brother of yours were surely a pair of misfits. Texas can breed 'em, an' that's a fact!"

"Did you ever meet a braver man than my brother Frank?" Brown inquired angrily.

"He was brave all right," Hasher scorned. "But you've got to be plumb stupid to be that brave!"

"Maybe so," Brown conceded, more

mollified than the words allowed. "He sure was a caution."

"Just be thankful you didn't have to baby that pack of loons, Jacko," Hasher sighed, half smiling. "Why, hell! Those were the best years. Weren't they so?"

"Huh," Brown grunted. "You about ready to stand up on your hindlegs and start shooting?"

"Fighting you is past me, Brown," Hasher said frankly. "Doubt I — I could lift my — my pistol. Want to do me a hand's turn — good or bad, as you please — by putting that gun of yours to my head and just pullin' the trigger?"

"Don't make a fuss now."

"That ain't worthy of you."

Brown sighed heavily, straight down through his nose; it wasn't worthy of him either. "Consumption?"

"You know it."

"Sounds like your sins have caught up with you, mister."

"Jack, there's nary a sin in me that's not in you too."

9

Brown poured his enemy a third whisky. "Sergeant, I'll drown you!"

"Not in that maid's water, you won't!" Hasher scoffed. "Jacko, I was born on them high Ozarks. Satan ran his first still in Tennessee."

"Sure, you're tough as old boots," Brown acknowledged. "But, give it a short while, and you'll be just as dead anyhow."

"Mebbe this is the right place for me to cash in," Hasher reflected. "Hellsgate, Kansas. What d'you say?"

"You can still see the funny side sure enough," Brown credited grudgingly. "You haven't lost your sense of humour, but you ought to have done. You must have heard about me doggin' you. It's been seven years."

"I heard somethin'," the ex-sergeant-of-cavalry admitted. "But I didn't take it too seriously. Had I done, I'd have been back with my rifle and put a slug in you."

"So you didn't pay much mind,"

Brown said tightly. "Well, damn your hide!"

"Didn't I make that plain?" Hasher inquired. "When first you came stormin' into this saloon and calling me out? Why, didn't all the folk go scurryin' — and there was no need."

"No need!"

"Guilty o' nothing, suh," the Tennessean explained. "Just plain sick — and tired. It was you forcing the fight. I never heard such misinformed hollerin'."

"Misinformed now!" Brown complained. "You and Tyson and the rest rode off. Wouldn't you say that was guilty enough?"

"I was guilty of nothing that night, Jacko," Hasher said evenly — "except trying to save my pals from what I believed then was a coming Yankee massacre. The Yanks sure didn't like us Tennessee boys. They had us figured for theirs, you see."

"Curse them!" Brown agreed. "Tennessee was true south."

"We didn't play the Kentucky game," Hasher said disdainfully, drinking now with relish rather than from need. "Weren't the boys; they was good as gold. But them politicians was traitors." He sniffed and set his empty glass aside. "Thankee, Jack; that was good. No, I didn't know a blamed thing about that stolen coin until a while afterwards. Too busy dodging bullets — our own and the Union's."

"It's incredible," Brown said, more to himself than the man seated at the card table. "I figured you were dodging *me* first as last. We can't tell — and never will — but did I just keep missing you at this place and that?"

"Appears so," Hasher commented. "They speak of Providence, hey? To crown it, I would have been gone from here the day before yesterday, but I heard the colonel was due in here with a herd up from the Red river country."

"The colonel? Riches? Clyde Riches?"

"Our colonel, yes. Riches of the

First Texas Cavalry. Our bunch. Big cattleman now."

"Heard something about that," Brown confessed. "As you do, getting around these parts. The trailherders often talk of him, high as Salina and Abilene. Have you seen him?"

"Last evening. Sure. Asked him for a job. And got one."

"I wonder he didn't lynch you," Brown reflected. "He had you pegged for guilty of running off with that Yankee payroll. Had a real old stamp about it. Even gave the names of you and Tyson, Dibber and the other two, to a Federal investigator. He called you renegades."

Hasher looked up sharply, appearing greatly surprised. "I lost touch with Abel Tyson, Jim Dibber, Mack Forder and Bill Lumley, in the fall of Sixty-five. I discovered last night those men have been riding for Clyde Riches since the spring of Sixty-eight, when the colonel brought his first herd north. All a matter of forgive and forget, eh? Riches never was a man to hold a grudge."

"Maybe not," Brown said doubtfully. "It don't sit right all the same. Riches was laying down the law to that Federal policeman in a criminal matter. Still, if they were innocent as you say — "

"As I was too," Hasher confirmed most emphatically. "It makes sense, doesn't it?"

"I guess so," Brown conceded, his brow still tight-knit. "Forgive and forget. That's got to be it. We can't go on carrying old grudges."

"It's you saying it," the Tennessean reminded seriously. "Jacko, for the last time — and as before God and Eternity — I had no hand in killing your brother Frank, and neither did the guys I led out of camp that night."

"Yet somebody made off with that Yankee payroll," Brown said heavily. "If you didn't have it, where did it go?"

"It's got me licked too."

"Who shot Frank?"

"Like as not, boy, you'll never know."

Brown touched the spot where his own head had been wounded. "The bullets were coming from the left of the fire, so I sat facing west."

"That was where Clyde Riches and Captain George Bayes had their tents," Hasher observed, coughing again and resuming the waxen transparency of cheek always associated with tubercular decline. "A lot of other guys were over that way, too, if it comes to that."

"Riches was *the* disciplinarian," Brown observed. "It's odd the hottest of that shooting should have come from his side of the camp."

"It was an odd sort of night," Hasher croaked through the thickness of his tubes. "The Union lived in that time, but the Confederacy died. In circumstances like that anything might happen. There was darkness in the vale of the temple, eh?"

"Heck of a way to put it," Brown

said, "but I reckon I follow you. Was it so holy?"

"We held it so."

"That we did, Hasher, but the world goes on."

"Forget it."

"I aim to do just that."

"And do what?"

"Like always, work," Brown replied. "Comes down to a job."

"I think I can get you one," Hasher returned. "Clyde Riches told me he needs another man. To help watch the holding grounds outside town. Seems he ain't due to load his herd for shipment before the end of next week."

"Sounds kind of temporary."

"Might not be," Hasher said, a wryly meaningful note in his voice. "The colonel said he'd take me back with him to work on his ranch in northern Texas. But you and me both know I ain't going to see out a ride like that."

"You might surprise yourself," Brown said comfortingly. "Guys have been known to get better from your complaint."

"But they mostly die," the consumptive ex-sergeant remarked bleakly. "Oh, to hell with it! You're doing right anyhow. If you'd dug my grave, like as not you'd have dug your own grave too."

"How's that?"

"Just thinkin' of what the Chinese say about revenge."

"The Chinks say a lot of things."

"First dig two graves."

Brown chuckled mirthlessly. "Two graves at Hellsgate, eh? Got a nice ring to it."

"Death knell, Jacko."

"At that, you never can tell."

"Let's go and see the colonel."

"All right," Brown said, quickening to the prospect and again feeling amazement at himself, for Hasher was still the man that, not fifteen minutes ago, he had hated through to the core and made a habit of gunning down every day for years in his imagination.

Yet here they were, the pair of them, chatting together like friends and ready to do each other favours. All at the prompting of a sudden trust based on the doubts of one and the relief of the other. For nothing had been tried or put to the test, and everything had happened with a minimum of soul-searching and emotional turmoil on his part. The change in him was hardly explicable. He ought to be furious at his own mental inconstancy. It was almost as if he were betraying his dead brother. As with that two graves business, a man also betrayed himself when he betrayed an oath. Yet it had often seemed to him that the human mind sometimes felt the truth and did not have to reason it. Whatever, there had been a change in him towards Marvin Hasher of the most sudden and significant kind and he could only go along with it in every meaning of the words. Then came an afterthought. "A toast before we leave."

"To what?" Hasher queried.

"All that I plan to forget," Brown replied, filling his companion's glass yet again and then lifting the bottle itself to his own mouth. "To what was, and all that could have been. To the South. May history not forget us!"

"Amen to that!" Hasher declared, emptying his glass at a single swallow. "Here's to the future also."

Brown nodded at Hasher's addition to the original toast. He took a second pull at his bottle in honour of it, and was in the act of setting down what remained of the rye whisky, when a gun flashed out of the shadows that traced the gallery high on the wall at the opposite side of the room and Hasher sat up sharply in his chair and gasped, clutching at his heart as he toppled sideways to the floor and came to rest with what could only be a lifeless thud.

2

Shocked rigid, Brown stood gaping upwards in the direction from which the shot had come. Then an abrupt movement in the shadows that had filled the length of the balcony above alerted him to a renewed threat, and he dropped instantly to his left knee and jerked his pistol, a second bullet arriving a split second later and tearing away part of his jacket collar. Still reacting on impulse, he fired back along the flash of the weapon above — thumbing and triggering with a practised speed — and sent three slugs whistling towards the shadows behind a heavy section of the balustrade at the edge of the walkway overhead that gave cover to his attacker.

The echoes of the gunfire rolled and throbbed about the man in the lower position, beating at his eardrums, yet, through this abuse of his hearing, Brown was sure that he picked up a gasp of pain. After that he saw a man's figure come abruptly erect in the upper gloom and go stumbling off to the right, this line of retreat giving the would-be killer almost instant access to a passage that served the bedrooms on the northern side of the saloon's upper floor.

Brown hesitated to give chase — since he doubted that it would have much chance of success — but his rage was greater than his good sense and, hearing a heavy tread in full flight up there, he whirled towards the balcony stairs and dived for a steadying grip at the foot of the right-hand rail. Then into the climb he went, taking the steps two at a time and ignoring the following yells of protest from the barkeeper and, reaching the balcony floor, he pelted to its further end and entered the passage down which the bushwhacker had fled.

Brown drove his legs to the limit.

Straining his ears above the noise of his own footfalls, he detected a tremoring of sound from what he judged to be the full extent of the building beyond him. Next he received the impression of his quarry jumping onto a backstair and beginning a clumsy descent towards ground level, the noises suggesting that the man ahead was heavily made and perhaps past his prime. There was hope in that, and Brown drew a new surge of energy from it.

He saw the end of the corridor rushing at him. Where the heck were those backstairs? There had to be a landing nearby. Then he saw it on his left, with the stairs descending steeply into a shadowy well beneath the single window at the passage's end. Onto the steps he sprang, turning his face up and round to offer a scowl as a door opened only yards in his wake and a young woman screamed after him. Now down he went, scampering, and then he felt a brief draught gust upwards into his face as a door at ground level — which obviously communicated with the outside — opened at speed and slammed shut even faster.

Seeing the bottom of the stairs just four steps below him, Brown leapt into space and came to rest on his soles in the hall, a thick mat reducing the impact. Recovering himself, he wrenched open the door before him and stumbled into the air, finding himself in an alleyway that connected the main street on his left with the saloon's back yard on his right. Under his feet was a step of grey slate, and upon this slab he saw a few flecks of blood. This appeared to confirm that he had indeed winged the killer back there in the bar-room, while a closer glance revealed that the faint red trail led off to the left and the main street itself.

Brown made for the street, legs flying as seldom before. Coming to the head of the alley, he checked, eyes peering first one way and then the other, and to his right he glimpsed a running figure in the act of ducking away into a passage on the same hand. Brown had no doubt that the man so briefly spotted was the bushwhacker. He raised his gun once more and took aim, figuring that the angle which now covered the fugitive was constructed of clapboard and little else, and that his forty-four calibre slugs would tear through it like so much paper, and he let fly for all he was worth, emptying his gun through the corner of the building at the alley's head with total venom — yet realizing that his action was more an expression of frustration than one likely to produce a result.

Cursing to himself, Brown stretched back into motion, determined to catch up with the vanished killer before all was done, but he hadn't covered half the forty yards between him and the alley into which the other had disappeared, when a huge figure stepped into his path out of a doorway on the right and a hand holding a sixgun swung at his head, the barrel of the weapon clipping his crown and dropping him to his knees, where he knelt sick at the belly and all but unconscious.

Brown wondered what in hell had happened. He strove to retain his grip on his whirling senses. Achieving that but little more, he was aware of a boot striking his upturned backside and flattening him along the sidewalk. Then his gun was torn out of his grasp and hurled into the doorway adjacent. After that he was heaved erect by hands that were truly strong and merciless and sent whirling towards a nearby horse-trough. His knees struck the edge of the trough and pitched his upper body forward into the water which the vessel contained, his face immersing and his arms doing the same. Nor was his assailant satisfied with just throwing him around like so much garbage; in fact the other seemed intent on extending the discipline to the limit. Gripping the back of his victim's neck, he shoved Brown's jaw to the bottom of the trough and held it there, drowning the struggling man by slow degrees; and Brown was all but kicking the last of his life away, when the giant in charge finally seemed to decide that enough was enough and snatched his face back into the air, letting him gather enough oxygen to begin coughing his throat and lungs clear before spinning him round and marching him into the building from which the big man's attack had appeared to commence. "I'll larn you!" the unknown declared gruffly. "I will not have guns fired on my streets!"

"Your streets?" Brown spluttered. "You King George or something?"

"I'm Sheriff Albert Lotus!" the other announced a trifle self-importantly. "I'm the law in Hellsgate!"

"Well, hell!" Brown croaked. "What a stinker!"

"You what, you what?" Lotus gobbled, picking him up and throwing him neck-and-crop into the middle of the three iron cages which crossed the back of the room which they had so recently

26

entered from the street. "Haven't you had enough?"

"Enough — enough!" Brown conceded. "It's you with all the appetite."

"Southern skunk!"

"That different from the Northern polecat?" Brown inquired.

"Shut up!"

"Peace, Sheriff!" Brown invoked, raising both hands as he squared round into a sitting position on the cell bunk onto which he had been thrown. "I only fired on somebody who'd already fired on me. Since when was that a crime?"

"Since you were damn fool enough to commit it," the big man replied uncompromisingly, his block of a jaw thrusting out of his rough-cut face. "If you got shot at, mister, you should have come and told me. I'd have done the shootin' back."

"Bit late when you're dead," Brown remarked.

"You get an average sort of funeral in this town."

"Sheriff, I can believe that."

"So what have you got doubts about, you rattletrap rebel scum?" Sheriff Lotus demanded, more than filling the doorway of Brown's cell. "Drover?"

"Not so's you'd notice," Brown sighed. "Well travelled, sir, and I've done this'n that."

"Who shot at you?"

"Can't put a name to him. Wish I could."

"Where was this?"

"Goodman's Long Bar," Brown replied. "The fellow who tried to kill me had already bushwhacked another man there."

"Killed him?"

"Dead."

Lotus drew himself up, square of chest and massive, his great nose ready to fall like an axe and the blood hot in his brick-red cheeks. "What? You gone luggy?"

"I'll kick your butt till you can't stand!"

28

"I can't do that now!" Brown protested. "You asked, and I answered. If there's thing I hate, it's repeating myself."

"Who got killed?"

"A guy named Marvin Hasher."

"Hasher, eh?" Lotus mused, showing his tombstone teeth as a muddy orb narrowed under an eyebrow. "What's your name, by the way?"

"Brown. Jack Brown."

"Brown, eh? You can't get more common than that. Yet it's familiar too. I wonder why?"

"A big clan, us Browns."

"There's a heap more to it than that, I think," the lawman said. "So long as you didn't kill him — "

"I didn't," Brown interrupted. "Yes, I'd hunted the guy for years, and would surely have put him in the undertaker's window if he'd been up to fighting; but he was bad sick — the consumption, y'know — and that gave us time to talk. When we'd done talkin', I knew there'd never been cause to fight and I

29

was ready to work with Marv instead. Makes you think, Sheriff."

"Sounds like a real story."

"It'd fill a book," Brown said reflectively. "This sure is a rare time to live in."

"What's wrong with it, jackass?" Lotus hectored.

"Mostly men like you," Brown returned evenly. "You have no right to hold me in here, Sheriff?"

"How many more times?" Lotus rasped. "You fired a gun on my street, and I don't need more right than that. I may even hold you for the circuit judge."

"That's crazy!" Brown declared. "It's wanton too!"

"Well, you're not leaving that cell until I'm sure what happened along at Goodman's."

"Pay a visit then," Brown encouraged. "It's due." The sheriff made to speak again, but there was sudden movement in the doorway of his office and he craned to see what it was, clearing his throat as a tall, open-faced young man came in and gave the new tin star on the front of his shirt a proprietorial rub. "Got news for you, Sheriff," he said. "There's been a killing along at Goodman's."

"That's no news to me, Buck," Lotus said, enjoying a moment's superiority over his deputy. "There's a good chance I've already got the man who did it in the lock-up. No beauty, is he? Anyhow, he's been shooting on the street — and you know I won't have that."

"Yeah," the youthful deputy said — "I know you won't have that. You going to do the questioning in Goodman's?"

"Shortly."

"The guy you've got there sure fits the description the barman gave."

"Jake Hansie's got a true eye," the sheriff observed. "Didn't Jake tell you anything past the fact of the killing?"

"If you've got the second man — "

"Did he say it was a bushwhacking?"

"Matter-of-fact he did," the deputy acknowledged; and he went on to provide much the same rather sketchy outline of the recent fatal doings at Goodman's as Brown had already given.

"I'll confirm it, Buck," Albert Lotus said, nodding. "What was the bad blood between you and Marvin Hasher, Brown? It went right back to the Civil War, didn't it?"

"To the very end," Brown answered, going on to tell the tale of that fateful night when his brother Frank had died in the sudden gunfire which had laced their Cavalry outfit's last camp of the war and of how Sergeant Hasher and those four troopers had galloped off, as he had for years supposed — though now believed, wrongly — with the Yankee payroll that he and the other men under Colonel Clyde Riches's command had captured during the day then ending. To give the account body, he added some detail concerning his search for Hasher in the years since the war, ending up with his regret for the time wasted and his sadness, too, for having been the fate which had dogged the sergeant up to the very hour of his death. "There you have it," he said finally, looking at the floor. "It don't sound like much now, but it almost seems to me there was never a time when I could hear anything else."

"That all of it?" Lotus asked.

"Every last word of it that matters," Brown assured him.

"What d'you think about it, young Colman?" the sheriff asked of his deputy.

"Don't sound to me like you've got the killer there, Albert," the deputy vouchsafed. "What he's just told us fits too well with what's happened and all else we've heard."

"He's not our man," Lotus admitted grudgingly.

"I shot at your man," Brown reminded, shaking his wet sleeve and otherwise shivering in his damp garments. "My pistol is lying there on the step. Mind if I pick it up and leave."

"You sit your ass down," the sheriff advised, "and let's hear no more about that." He indicated that his deputy should pick up the mentioned Colt and place it on the office desk; then, his brow furrowing, he went on: "I recall that business about the Army payroll now. The gold was never recovered. I reckon Washington is still sick as a toad about it. Makes you wonder who the thief was. I mean, if Hasher had no finger in it, why would anybody have wanted to murder him — or this man, Brown, if it comes to that?"

"Got to be a matter of shutting mouths," the deputy mused. "There's either fear or uncertainty somewhere."

"Both," Brown said. "Marv Hasher knew nothin', and I know the same. The real mystery remains, and my brother's killer is still running free."

"Sooner or later it will all come out," Sheriff Lotus said confidently.

"It could have been sooner," Brown reminded, his tones unforgiving. "I might still have nailed the son-of-a bitch who did the deed in Goodman's if you hadn't knocked me over and put me in the water."

Lotus gave Brown an almost feral glare. "Lock him up, Buck! I'll larn him!"

"Okay, Sheriff," the deputy said — "but is that wise?"

"Wise?"

"You know how this town can be," Colman answered, a reminder in his voice. "Only right to warn you — "

"You don't warn me of anything, boy," the giant sheriff cautioned. "I said to lock him up."

"Yes, sir," the younger lawman responded, lifting a ring of keys from the cluttered top of the office desk and carrying it over to the cage in which Brown still sat. Then he shut the cell door and, after selecting the key that fitted, turned the lock on the prisoner. Finally he threw the key-ring back so that it landed upon the desktop at almost the spot from which he had taken it.

After that Sheriff Lotus passed out of the street door. "I'll be back before long," he said across his shoulder. "Watch him. You're responsible, mind."

"Yeah, yeah," Buck Colman agreed to himself.

"Hey, what's up with this town?" Brown demanded uneasily.

"Oh, nothing to get het up about," Colman answered, moving between the windows in the front wall of the room and testing the heavy shutters there. "There's a need to be watchful, that's all. Not so long ago, this town had a reputation for lynching its killers. We've had a killing and, as you're the only prisoner we've got, somebody might get to thinking about the old ways — before Albert Lotus took over." His inspection of the shutters completed, the deputy walked to the desk and sat down, shooting his legs into the knee-hole and tipping his weight against the back of the chair. "You'll be all right. I'm here."

Abruptly chilled, Brown found little comfort in the deputy's reassurance and he stretched out on his back and began to see pictures behind his eyes that he could have done without.

3

It was soon clear to the apprehensive Brown that Deputy Sheriff Buck Colman was not usually a talkative type — not where prisoners were concerned anyhow — and he found that he could raise no further word from the young man who had been left in charge of him. This being so, he was forced, after one or two abortive attempts to renew Colman's interest, to literally sit looking out through the bars of his cell and twiddling his thumbs.

Brown felt disgruntled and impotent. Everything was at sixes and sevens. He simply could not square the logic of the day with what was now happening to him. He was being treated like a criminal for no worse than trying to defend himself — even trying, in some sense, to do the law's job for it. What had happened to fairness and decency, if they had ever existed in his world? Yet he knew in his heart of hearts that it was no good looking for better treatment than he was getting now. That hulking varmint, Sheriff Lotus, had him all ends up and was covering the angles. Punishment was being made to confound innocence and at the same time to protect. There was nothing happening here of which a judge would not approve. Yet it was equally true that, to a vengeful onlooker, his treatment must have a taint of guilt to it. If a mob should come baying for his blood, the participants in his murder could also be excused their act. Rough justice did the job, and prejudice had never held a trial. The irony of it all!

Eyeing the round-faced clock that hung upon the wall over the office fireplace, Brown was convinced that the clunking old timepiece only measured one minute in every two. The afternoon was dragging by, and Sheriff Lotus seemed to be taking an inordinate amount of time to do relatively little.

How many questions did you need to confirm a straightforward story? All the lawman had to do was return and free his prisoner. The suspense would then seep out of this business, and he, Brown, could look after his own safety. If the need was there, he could do a better job of running than most. In fact he'd be glad to shake the dust of Hellsgate off his feet in any circumstances. Dammit! Where was that consarned sheriff? Had he fallen down the privy?

Even the taciturn Buck Colman appeared to begin losing patience. The deputy rose from his chair and started to slowly pace the front of the office. Every now and again he would glance out of the window to the left of the door and look along the street, sniffing just audibly on each occasion. Then his feet would resume their plodding.

"Why don't you sit down again, boy?" Brown finally demanded. "You're giving me grey hairs!"

"Could improve your looks," Colman

opined, rising to the bait this time. "What's up with you?"

"Fed up with this," Brown replied bluntly. "That boss of yours sure takes his time. Wouldn't you say?"

"He ain't accountable to me — or you," the deputy reminded. "Did you never find yourself with something that took longer to do than you expected?"

"Every day," Brown admitted. "Unlock me. Let me come out there with you."

"And get sent home with my ass in a sling?"

"Goldurn charade!"

"We'll see, won't we?"

"You've already acknowledged it, Colman."

"Do I have to practise what — ?" The deputy broke off, his face set and ear listening, for the thudding of a big bass drum was suddenly audible from way down the street. "Oh, no! Hell — no!"

"What's that?" Brown asked. "It sounds like the town band."

"Would to heck that was the whole if it!" Colman gritted. "It's that blamed Hannah Riker and her support."

"Who's Hannah Riker?"

"If she'd been born a man," the deputy responded, "me and Albert Lotus would have ridden her out of town on a rail long ago. But the evil old troublemaker was born a woman, and that makes all the difference." He made a ball of the bad taste in his mouth and looked as if he were about to spit. "Widow Riker, d'you see? That's where she gets her sympathy from. Her husband got gunned down a few years ago. He was a hoss thief, and it was no more than he deserved. But it's been the widow's excuse for incitin' lynch mobs ever since. She's always listening at our door for a chance to stir the pot. I'd say she's heard of today's killing and how we've got you lodged in the calaboose. Any excuse will do!"

"I'm due to be strung up?" Brown yelped.

"Sounds like it," the deputy said

rather helplessly. "Listen to that band! Hannah is sure on the march!"

"I'll see Albert Lotus in hell!" Brown ground out.

"You won't see him any place else," Colman allowed.

"Let me out of here," Brown insisted, "and give me my gun back."

"Keep your skull down and hold your row," Colman advised, going to the street door and shooting the lock, then dropping the retaining bar into place also. "Pray for the best, but be ready for the worst. This could prove no more than the widow and her pals letting off steam."

Brown turned his eyes to the ceiling. He felt like running round his cage in circles, cursing God and Man, and he certainly didn't feel like banking on the off chance. In his experience, if the worst was threatening, it usually happened. Last minute deliverance did occur, but it invariably benefited somebody else.

The band drew on. Colman turned to

43

face the blaring music, and Brown did the same. The trombones brayed, and the drum went on thudding. Louder and louder grew the noise. Then the brazen cacophony — and the folk responsible for it — fetched up in the street outside, visible to the deputy sheriff and prisoner within the law office through either window. The band hit fortefortissimo, its shredded rendition of 'Marching Through Georgia' just recognisable, then came to a thumped conclusion and moments of profound silence followed.

Suddenly there was a crash of breaking glass as a window flew to pieces and a stone sailed in from the street. It bruised a corner of the sheriff's desk, spun across the floorboards, and clattered to rest at the foot of the bars that imprisoned Brown. "Woe unto you, foul shedder of blood!" bawled a voice that had more in common with a vulture's than a human female's. "Art thou, then, Cain, murderer of thy brother? Hide thy face, O son of shame, for thou mayest be sure that the Lord thy God will visit upon thee the punishment of hell before the hour is gone. Even now the wrath of the Almighty reaches out for thee, O wicked man, and the pain of His vengeance is closing upon thee. Hear me, O son of the Slime, for I am the tongue of Jehovah and hold His sword above thy — "

"It looks more like a coil of rope to me, Hannah!" Colman shouted back through the broken window. "You come over here a minute!"

"What do you want, Buck Colman?" the vulturine voice demanded.

Now Brown had his first clear view of Hannah Riker. She appeared at the window behind which the deputy was standing. Brown saw at once that the woman was not old in the true meaning of the word. It was simply that her cheeks were so hollow and her grey hair so wispy that fifty on her looked like seventy, while her rusty black garments, covering a body that ran straight up and down, suggested a scarecrow newly home from work. That Hannah was intrinsically wicked, Brown had no doubt — and that she would rejoice in standing by while others stretched his neck, he was certain — but he was likewise sure that she must be an object of derision in any company of normally intelligent people; so he felt that his best hope must be to attempt to guide the deputy into getting a rise out of her and thus perhaps diluting the harm that she was here to do. "Don't stand there flapping like a flea-bit old hen!" he called to her. "The boy wants a dollar for that window you smashed. Pay up, Hannah!"

"Shan't!" The harridan stamped her left foot hard. "Can't!"

"Can't?" Brown echoed in disbelief. "You've gotta. Go and sell your funeral suit!"

Peering inwards, the woman in black shook a fist. "I'll give it to you, child of Satan!"

"Seems my day to go up in the

world," Brown reflected, conscious already of laughter out in the street, "whether I like it or not. The devil won't own me, Hannah. Says he wasn't to blame the day I was begot. Shame on you for bearing false witness! Why, you'll have me calling you mama next!"

"Have you no respect for a poor widder woman?" Hannah Riker wailed. "I won't put no flowers on your — "

"Hold your row, Hannah!" bawled a voice that Brown recognised as Sheriff Lotus's from a short distance along the street; and then metal rang and jangled as a powerful hand took a crowbar to the alarm triangle which Brown had seen framed at the approaches to the fire depot when he had entered Hellsgate that morning. "Scat, the lot of you!" Lotus went on, at a break in the teeth-clenching clamour. "Get off the street, Mrs Riker, and take those idiot musicians with you! I'll put the lot of you into the cells if we have any more of it! Go! And I do mean right now!" Again the triangle rang out its cautionary message.

It was already plain how thoroughly Sheriff Lotus was feared in town. People were already fleeing in the direction opposite to that which he occupied, Hannah Riker pumping her arms upwards and squawking in their midst. Bending, Buck Colman pushed his face closer to the shattered glass and slapped his thighs, laughing with boyish glee. "That's fixed her waggon!" he declared. "Pesky old bird!"

"Yeah," Brown agreed humorously, though he was mightily relieved all the same, "I'll swear I last saw her flying over the field at Shiloh." He glanced at the door. "Hadn't you better unlock this place again? Your boss will want to come in shortly."

Nodding, Colman moved quickly to the door, first removing the retaining bar and then unlocking it. He had barely completed doing this, when the woodwork burst inwards and the giant shape of Albert Lotus entered, brow like the proverbial thundercloud but a look of satisfaction in his grim eyes nevertheless. Behind the sheriff walked a swart, square man who was almost as tall as he and of the sternest ambience. The newcomer glanced at once towards the cells, passing a black, button-bright eye over the prisoner, and he half smiled and nodded curtly, twitching at both ends of his waxed mare's-tail moustache as Sheriff Lotus said: "I understand you know this gentleman, Brown."

"Colonel Riches!" Brown acknowledged in a slightly startled voice, coming to attention as his deeper self remembered the drills of yesteryear. "Good afternoon, sir!"

"Well met, Brown," the colonel responded easily. "Been having a little fun, eh?"

"Wouldn't call it exactly that," the prisoner confessed.

"I expect not," Riches said. "How are you these days, my man?"

"I'll feel a sight better when I get the right side of these bars, sir."

"Dear me!" Riches reflected, lifting an eyebrow at the sheriff.

"Let him out of there, Buck," Lotus ordered; and the deputy moved to the office desk and picked up the key-ring again, walking then to the cells and freeing the man imprisoned in the middle of the three cages.

Brown emerged from his cell. "Thankee, Sheriff," he said. "We wondered what had become of you. Now we know."

"Yes, I went out to the holding grounds at the railhead," Lotus said. "It had occurred to me — from what you'd told us about Marvin Hasher and soldiering — that Colonel Riches might be the man to solve the problem you presented."

"Glad to be of service, Sheriff," Riches declared heartily. "Big shock about Sergeant Hasher, but I'll be glad to take Brown south in his place. If Brown wants to come."

"He wants to," Lotus said a trifle darkly.

Tightening his mouth slightly, Brown gave a dutiful nod.

"Once a man has served with me," the colonel said, "he's welcome for life. I remember you as a good trooper, Brown, and I don't toss bouquets around."

"Thank you, sir," Brown responded. "Marv Hasher was going to bring me to your camp. The idea was to ask you to give me a job."

"Makes the best possible sense," Colonel Riches observed. "A happy outcome — almost. I know there was bad blood of long-standing between you and the sergeant, but I've heard enough to realize you and he had sorted it out. So you chased him for seven years, eh — intending to kill him every mile of the way — but ended up shaking hands? War makes its stories all right." He pressed reflectively on a leaky sinus. "Hasher was about finished, you know."

Brown jerked his chin. "I know the consumption when I see it."

"Well, the poor devil clearly had another deadly enemy besides yourself," Riches commented. "I reckon the sheriff will be lucky if he ever catches the killer."

"That man and I exchanged shots in the Long Bar," Brown said, "and I winged him."

"Forget about that," Riches said sharply, casting the sheriff a significant glance. "I'll take you to a new life down in Texas. As for that payroll business, it concerned me far more than you. I've forgotten about it, and you must do the same. It was hard luck about your brother, but think of how many died in that war. Life goes on, Brown."

"If you say so, Colonel," Brown said rather woodenly.

"Others fell in that random shooting. There was panic."

"I got the impression somebody was shooting with a purpose — and mighty straight — and I still have it."

"So forget about it!" Riches snapped. "Like it or not, you have to start again.

You know what they say about a gift horse?"

"I'm not going to throw the bit, Colonel," Brown promised. "It's my habit to look closely and to ask what's what. I can't change the man I am."

"All right, all right," Riches acknowledged dismissively. "A straight word at the start is best, hey?" He chuckled dryly. "I guess I've been jumping the gun by a sight. We can't leave Hellsgate before the end of next week. My cattle have still to be loaded on the railroad."

"Hasher told me about that, sir," Brown remarked. "It could embarrass me a bit if there's any repetition of what you saw just now."

"Detail," the colonel said, shrugging. "Just keep your head down. You'll have the crew around you. The camp's a mile out of town anyway."

"Behave yourself," Albert Lotus confirmed sternly, "and you've nothing to worry about."

"I'll be a model," Brown promised

firmly, "if I'm let be."

"You going to stand yapping for the rest of the day, Brown?" Riches inquired heartily. "I wish I had your jaw."

"Yours to command, sir," Brown assured him with due respect.

"We're on our way then, mister."

But the sheriff pointed towards his desk and said: "Don't forget your gun, Brown."

Brown and the colonel went for the pistol together, both moving fast, but the owner of the weapon got there first and palmed the Colt towards his holster.

"Let me have it," Riches suggested. "You can get into trouble if you're carrying a gun."

"But I can't get out of it if I'm not," Brown reminded, letting the revolver settle to rest deep in leather.

For an instant the colonel's smile was that on the face of a tiger; but it sweetened abruptly as he made for the street door.

Brown followed the man, frowning inwardly. Riches seemed to be trying a mite too hard. Now why would he do that? There could be reasons — both good and bad — but Brown wasn't prepared to credit any of them just then.

4

After turning left on the sidewalk, Brown and the colonel quickly put the law office behind them.

"What have you done with your horse, Brown?" Riches asked, as they passed the fire depot and Goodman's saloon and the Emporium came up on the left, garish in their rough paints and crude carpentry. "Did you put it in the livery stables?"

"It's standing outside the Long Bar," Brown answered.

"Good man," the colonel approved. "That's where I left my mount when I rode in with the sheriff."

They reached the hitching rail outside Goodman's. A fair number of horses had been tethered there in recent hours and the two men had to sort their animals from among the variety of mounts that drooped patiently along the splint, stepping up when they had untied and backed the creatures into the middle of the street. After that they rode slowly westwards — Riches's rangy bay and Brown's bob-tailed grulla seeming to communicate as little as their masters now did — and they soon put the built-up area behind them and came to a broad view of the prairie and the lately constructed railhead which dominated the nearer ground with its engine sheds, water tower, stockpens and ramps, wired-in holding areas, and threadbare cowcamps over which the smoke of cooking fires curled greyly. All this without mentioning the tens of thousands of cattle which blackened the scene in a confusion of ever-shifting detail while echoing incessantly with the lowing of the herds.

It was now the briefest of rides into the cattle area, and soon over. Trotting parallel with the scene, Brown was impressed by the size of it and the numbers involved, but little else. He had worked cows often enough, to make eating money, but had no love of them, and their stink turned his stomach. It was simply that you did what you had to in order to stay alive, and he was on that tack again. Only a fool expected to feel the inspiration of great things, and the wise man just let it happen. Sure, he was at another crossroads, but there had been plenty of those in his life. There were guys watching him idly — scruffy, ill-dressed fellows, just like him — and it was required that he sing small and make himself agreeable. He was determined to do just that. Hell, he'd always been a good comrade, hadn't he? He doubted that the difference between the cowcamp and the bivouacks was really that great.

The Riches Rocking R outfit had its place on the most westerly of the Hellsgate holding grass. Moving into the camp at the colonel's side, Brown kept a grin on his face and flipped good-natured salutes around him, for there were faces everywhere that he remembered from his Army days. Prominent among them were those of George Bayes, once captain of C Troop and the colonel's aide-de-camp — now, as Riches so swiftly explained, the Rocking R's ramrod and still a man to be obeyed — that of the hard-lipped Abel Tyson, an unloved corporal of horse and one of the four soldiers who had deserted on that fateful night of the payroll theft, and those of the fat and shifty Bill Lumley, the slack-seated Mack Forder, and the hot-eyed, vaguely threatening Jim Dibber, the other three men who had kept Tyson and Sergeant Hasher company on that occasion. There were Menzies, Forbes, Reaper and Cullenden, too — lesser lights, but remembered for this and that — and 'Big Roger' Clunes, the colonel's servant. Nor did he miss John Bagle and Fabian Lessing, officers both, though the latter was a lean, lynx-eyed aristocrat who was said to have done murder in high society before the war. Indeed, it appeared to Brown that all the important members of the wartime band were there, and that, though the uniforms had been exchanged for Stetsons and range duds, Clyde Riches could still summon his men as readily by the trumpet call as a shout round the bunkhouse door. It was reassuring — even heartening — but there were a few dark looks too. Some trouble would come, he was certain of that, but when had the life of a common man ever been all plain sailing?

Riches ordered Brown to halt and dismount when they reached the chuck waggon. "Feed this man," he ordered, as the cook stuck his head out of the canvas door at the vehicle's back. "He's one of us now."

"Yes, sir, colonel!" the cook responded from beneath a walrus moustache that appeared the largest feature on his shrivelled, wind-blasted face.

"You, Brown," Riches went on, shifting his gaze without turning his chin — "come to my tent when you've eaten. There are one or two formalities we should observe."

Brown touched his forelock, then washed a good meal down with a mug of even better coffee; and after that he located the colonel's tent and went inside, seeing immediately that Riches was in conference with a pasty-cheeked and altogether seedy-looking George Bayes, who was slumped on a camp stool and pulling morosely at a cold pipe. 'Big Roger' Clunes and Fabian Lessing were also present; but the one just stood there, while the other appeared to be reflecting on the length of his fingernails.

"Ah, there you are, Brown!" the colonel said. "George Bayes and I have just been discussing you. You've eaten well?"

"Never better."

"That's what I like to hear," Riches approved. "Eat well, work well. We all muck in together. When the going gets tough, it's share and share alike on my ranch at High Plains, Texas. For the rest, the business is pretty much like any other. I pay a dollar-fifty a day all found. At round-up, the brand supplies the remounts. You get Sundays off on a rotating basis, and there's an annual bonus — when the profits justify it." He paused, eyes questioning. "Does it satisfy you, Brown? Is there anything you don't like?"

"It'll suit me fine," Brown replied. "Sounds a better deal than most get."

"All in the family," Riches said expansively. "Do you want to add anything, George?"

"Brown knows me — and what I expect of a man," George Bayes remarked, giving an audible gasp of pain and dropping his pipe from between his teeth as 'Big Roger' Clunes turned to pick up a pencil which Riches had just let fall and caught the ex-captain with a buttock. "Damn you, Clunes!"

"Real sorry, Mr Bayes!" the enormous Clunes bleated, returning the colonel's pencil. "Wasn't looking, I guess."

"Not at me," the thick-set Bayes

agreed sourly. "Be more careful!"

"George!" the colonel barked, glancing swiftly at his ramrod with an expression of reproof that seemed more surprised from him than needed.

Something in Brown alerted, but he couldn't tell exactly what. Now he passed a more discerning eye over the ex-captain than he had done previously. It occurred to him then that Bayes, although looking much below par, had taken the trouble to spruce himself up, a general need that did not appear to have crossed any other mind present. The colonel's right-hand man was wearing a clean grey shirt and a new jacket, items which, it had to be admitted, the filthy life around the camp hardly encouraged. It was not important, of course — since there was no law against breaking in new garments where dirt made ruin almost immediate — but it was curious and made Brown concentrate quickly on the right cuff that Bayes seemed to snatch into hiding. "You hurt, Cap'n?" he inquired, an impossible thought rising in his mind and refusing to die quite as readily as it should have done. "Did I see blood?"

"You may've done," Bayes said reluctantly, his manner brusque. "Blamed bubwire. I hate the stuff!"

"We all do, Cap'n," Brown assured him. "Those barbs do wicked damage if you run up against 'em. Can ruin a horse."

Bayes scowled, but Riches smiled — if, as was normal for him, a little sardonically — and he said: "These things are sent to try us. That will be all, Brown."

Nodding, Brown touched his forelock, then turned and ducked towards the tent floor, pausing again as he sensed a movement from the man who had just dismissed him that expressed a sudden afterthought.

"One thing, Brown."

"Colonel?"

"Ready for work?"

"Right now if you want."

64

"You can ride our fence tonight," Riches advised — "from eight o'clock until midnight. It may appear an unnecessary chore, but it has to be done. There are always jumpers that we have to keep off the next man's grass."

"I can manage that right enough, sir," Brown said.

"Very well then. You'll share the duty with Roger Clunes."

"'Big Roger', sure," Brown confirmed, passing outside again and walking to where the supply waggon was chocked up and he had left his horse ground-tied. A bench had been provided and stood in the vehicle's shadow. It had clearly been put there for the use of the weary, and Brown sat down upon it. Then, folding his arms, he shut his eyes and began to doze, feeling the need to get a little shut-eye against the spell of night duty which had just been ordered for him. He feared that he might not be allowed to rest — with so many old and probably curious acquaintances nearby — but in fact nobody disturbed him and he was allowed to sink from dozing into sleep and dream pleasantly enough until a big hand shook him roughly awake and he opened his eyes once more to find 'Big Roger' Clunes looking over him and frowning belligerently. "What the deuce!" he spluttered rather stupidly. "We on, Roger?"

Clunes spat at Brown's feet. "Figured you'd lost track," he said disgustedly. "You were snoring like a drunk bullfrog."

"Hell, no."

"Hell, yes."

Brown's jaws rubbered and his arms stretched.

"Get your horse, then, and let's get to it."

"I hear you, Roger," Brown said, holding down a surge of temper as he rose to his feet and tugged the creases out of his rucked up trousers. Then, feeling more comfortable, he went to his horse and looked around it, checking his bit and belly girth, and finally he kicked aside the chunk of rock that anchored its reins to the ground and swung up, trotting over to join Clunes, who was sitting erect in leather and waiting for him beside the gate in the nearby fence which gave access to the Rocking R holding grass.

After studying him and his horse for a moment, 'Big Roger' tossed up a mocking laugh and asked: "Where'd you get that crowbait from?"

"He does his turn," Brown said shortly.

"Aye, like master like horse," Clunes mocked, plainly conscious of his own protective mass and, as ever, hardly caring for the feelings of others. "Well, there you are. You can see over the fields, Jack. The fences don't take much tracing. I'll ride round them from the right, and you do the same from the left. That way we'll keep criss-crossing out yonder and every inch of the ground will get regular attention."

"Simple enough," Brown acknowledged, gazing into the glare which sprang from the dark horizon where the sun's red ball was starting to set. "It'll be midnight before we know it."

"Can't be too soon for me," Clunes admitted distastefully. "I'm off. Sing to the critters if you want to, but spare me, hey?"

Grinning mechanically, Brown turned his horse away and began riding the fence. Clunes was Clunes, he supposed, and would have to be tolerated. His roughness was part of the cow country knock-about anyway. He was sure that he could whip the big guy if he had to, but why risk getting hurt over a few insults? Sticks and stones — !

Brown settled to the job, and his horse did likewise. Both knew all about the boredom of the ride and how to endure it. Around them the soft winds of the prairie soughed and the shadow of the night drew on, the last of the afterglow dying finally into the skyline and leaving a livid streak under the

68

western clouds. Time after time Brown trotted his horse round to the east and back again, careful to keep his eyes on the lift throughout. But nothing happened to alter the even tenor of his shift. No cow jumped the fence, and no bird flew at him out of the gloaming. Peace hung over the bed-grounds like a tangible presence, and presently a three-quarter moon swung up and chased off the threatening blackness, while patterns of white stars splashed and faded where the rack drifted. Stretching his legs against the stirrups, Brown wished that he had one of those Swiss turnips that chimed the hours, for he had no measure of the time — and the faint irritation he felt kept bringing to mind George Bayes and that blood on the man's wrist. Did Bayes have a chipped shoulder that was bleeding down his right arm? It had certainly looked like it. Yet the wound did not have to be a bullet wound, and even if it were, the bullet need not have come from his, Brown's pistol. Nevertheless, somebody had bushwhacked Marvin Hasher and — well — the connection of a past relationship, however tenuous, could mark down the cap'n for the guy responsible and open up all manner of ominous questions. The connection seemed too improbable for words, but the unlikely often turned out to be the truth.

It was about then that Brown heard a pair of horses drubbing in from windward and his idling mind alerted to present happenings again.

5

Gaze lowered and intent, Brown made out the silhouettes of the riders and mounts breasting the moonlight about a minute later. Slowing his own horse to the barest walk, he placed his presence directly in the path of the oncoming riders. But it seemed that the pair failed to detect his shape against the contours under the moon, for they reined in with cries of obvious shock and surprise when he shouted: "Who goes there? You're nigh into cattle, dammit!"

"What's that?" demanded a voice carrying sudden anger.

"You heard, mister!" Brown rejoined, touching his holster. "Come on up!"

The two riders approached at a wary trot, and their ashen outlines firmed up in the lunar glow and the voice of the man who had spoken previously — he

71

on the left — now asked: "Who are you? Mouth off some, don't you?"

"Aw, simmer down!" Brown advised disgustedly. "Don't keep fiddling with that hogleg. I'm just a man on herd watch. Don't go upsettin' the cows — please!"

"Okay, okay," the other said shortly, and he and his companion stopped their horses a yard or two from where Brown had also come to a halt. "We're the Parker brothers — Joe and Sammy — from down Evergreen way. I'm Joseph."

"Hi, boys!" their challenger acknowledged. "Jack Brown. Texas man myself."

"We got business here, Brown. We're looking for a man?"

"Who?"

"Colonel Clyde Riches," the second Parker brother now put in. "If he ain't arrived in hell yet."

"Some hopes of that!" brother Joseph scoffed. "Shut up, Sammy, and leave this to me."

"Yes, sir," Sammy sniffed.

Brown realized that he had tensed up considerably. These two had no liking for the colonel. That much was obvious, and concern enough. "I work for the colonel," he said as quietly as he could. "You can see his campfire over my left shoulder. What do you want with him?"

"Our business," Joe Parker confided.

"You sound riled as a hornet."

"We are riled. And not without cause."

"Like what?"

"Still our business, feller."

"Must allow," Brown responded reasonably. "I have to do my job, boys."

"Do it," Joe Parker advised uncompromisingly. "Ride the fence."

"You're making this tough," Brown sighed.

"It can get tougher," Joe Parker reminded. "We're two against one. Best let us by."

"Come to that," Brown said, "I don't

73

want any piece of work. Your business is your business, and the colonel's is his. Go and talk to him for all me."

"That's better," Joe Parker said.

Brown got his horse out of the way, and the brothers rode past him; but he was still looking after them across his shoulder, when 'Big Roger' Clunes rode up and said gruffly: "Who was that you were talking to?"

"Two brothers named Parker."

Clunes grunted to himself. "The Parker boys, eh? What did they want?"

"They wouldn't say. You know them, Roger?"

"You're some blamed good, Jack!"

"They wanted to speak with Clyde Riches, and that's what they've gone to do." Brown cocked a snook at the big man, stung despite himself. "Sounds to me like you've got a heck of a lot more idea of what it's all about than I have. Been up to no good, have you?"

"Don't talk so soft, man!"

"You must know," Brown growled at his pommel; then gigged up, speaking again as he passed Clunes. "Wonder what I've hired into, eh? It's a long way up from the Red River, and you could've whipped up a whole mess of badness while coming here." Please God the past wasn't the mirror of the future, for Clyde Riches and his outfit had always been trouble personified. Yet he knew it couldn't be otherwise. "Bless you, Roger, and may your rabbits die!"

Clunes swore after him, and they went on with their work, each avoiding the other by a wide margin whenever they passed again; but midnight soon came and their reliefs appeared; and Brown, having contemplated large trials in his imagination, rode back into camp thanking God for small mercies. At least it appeared that the Parker boys had come and gone and no blood had been spilled; so perhaps the nature of their grievances had not been so great after all.

Brown drank a cup of coffee at the cook's night fire; then, yawning, he unshipped his bedroll from behind his cantle and spread it in a free corner which he located under the supply waggon. After that he stretched out and spent a minute staring at the floor of the vehicle above him, willing sleep to come; then, having instructed his subconscious mind to awaken him at sunrise, he went back to his evening dreams and expected to remain at rest for several hours to come; thus it was quite a shock to him when he was shaken out of his sleep while night was still upon the camp and he heard the voice of 'Big Roger' Clunes breathe in his ear: "Roll out of it, sonny boy — we're off home."

"Home?" Brown mouthed blankly.

"Texas, damn your eyes!"

"But I thought — "

"So did we all," Clunes interrupted, never more abrupt. "There's been a change of plan. The colonel has arranged for our herd to be looked after by a local outfit for the rest of the time. They'll see to the loading of our cattle cars and any extra feeding and watering."

"That's okay by me," Brown said, forcing himself wide awake. "It makes me ask why, that's all."

"Never ask why on the Rocking R," Clunes advised; "just do it. What kind of soldier are you, Jack?"

"The civilian kind, big man."

"They get shot, too, when they don't obey orders," Clunes cautioned darkly. "Move your assend, thickhead!"

Brown drew himself out of his blankets. He said no word more, and watched Clunes, looming and ogreish against the paling glow of the not far distant campfire, slouch off to another part of the site. Then Brown pulled his blankets into the open and rolled them up again, returning his bed to the back of his cantle and tying it on once more. He was aware of much movement around him by this time, and smelled coffee, new bread and bacon on the go, and he picked up the word that was travelling from man to man that he should go to the chuck waggon and stuff himself while the opportunity was there, since grub would be in short supply once they got on the move and an empty belly was about the worst company that a riding man could keep. Primed thus, Brown led his mount to a position near the chuck waggon, leaving it with reins hanging while he ate and drank his fill, and after that he hung about on the fringe of things while the camp was flattened and the tents and furniture packed away. At sunup the outfit was ready to move, and it departed without further delay, clearing the Hellsgate district before anybody knew that it was gone and soon following the wide, worn cattle trail which would eventually bring them back to the Red River basin and the plains of home.

For hour after hour the haste was maintained. Colonel Riches would permit no slowing down. He communicated the urgency he felt by constant shouts and gestures from the front of his galloping party. The only pause he permitted — and that almost too brief to register — was for the watering of the waggon wheels and the greasing of their hubs, since you could not move as they were moving without bearings running hot and spokes starting to shrink within their iron tyres. It was pretty frantic, and the horses, driven to the point of safety, were a-sweat all the time. Dust, stink, and vanishing miles were the order of the day and, at a loss for the need to journey in this crazy fashion, Brown could only curse his leader and live with his bewilderment — and fear. For haste like this could only carry a threat to life behind it.

Even at sundown there was no let up and, as the day had gone, so went the first hours of the night. Men and animals had long been ready to drop, and Brown was amazed at how many stages of exhaustion flesh and blood could pass through and still carry on; but there was a final limit and, with the rising of the moon, it was apparent from the raggedness of the movement on all hands that collapse was imminent. Some light timber appeared before them just then and, when they reached the northern edge of it, Colonel Riches at long last signalled the halt and ordered a fire to be lighted and food prepared. They would rest, he announced, until dawn, then put in another long and hard day tomorrow. It amazed Brown that nobody protested — since the pace must eventually prove more than flesh and blood could stand — but then he judged that the men around him knew far more than he did and were undoubtedly sustained by the same fear that was driving the colonel. It was now apparent that something said by the Parker brothers last night must be behind this flight, and Brown was determined that presently he would go along to Riches and find out what it was. What had this bunch of misfits done on their cattle drive into Kansas? He felt that he had the right to know.

Brown stood his horse to one side,

then slumped down on the ground beside it, too worn out and disgruntled to even approach the fire — once it was lighted — or collect his share of the sandwiches handed out from the back of the chuck waggon. He didn't mind being pushed — that was all part of the game — but there had to be a reason for it that was good and acceptable. Otherwise he was burning up his life at a sinful waste and better on his own again. And perhaps that was the answer to it. Maybe he should slip away during the night. There was nothing here to bind him, and men who consorted with sinners often got punished for sins they hadn't committed.

A heel crunched on Brown's right. He looked quickly towards the sound. George Bayes was standing there. The ex-captain of horse was hunched and accusing under the tree-rippled moonlight. "I've been keeping my eye on you, Brown," he said. "What are you sulking over here for?"

"It's been a hard day, and I'm tired."

"It's been the same for all of us."

"With the difference that you've known what it's all about — and I haven't."

"You presume, mister," Bayes said coldly. "You amount to a heap of horse muck around here."

"I'm a hired man, Mr Bayes, and I have the right to some respect."

"Do you indeed?" the ex-captain sneered. "You've got a mile above yourself."

"We're running away from something," Brown insisted, getting to his feet and facing the other. "That's obvious."

"What gives you that idea?"

"I was the man who directed the Parker boys into camp last night."

"What did they tell you?"

"Nothing — as such," Brown answered. "That's the trouble. It was their frame of mind that's had me wondering. Those two were real angry."

"So what, Brown?" Bayes asked dismissively. "I can do without this — this impertinence."

"Ditto, Mr Bayes. But there's a time and place for all to be revealed — and I reckon our time and place is here."

"You're being paid to do as you're told. I could quote articles."

"You're as bad as that great loon Clunes," Brown said deliberately. "We're not playing armies any more. If I don't hear from you what I want to hear, I'm going to the colonel, and that's that."

"You've said it. He'll kill you."

"Some of the men might not like that," Brown reminded. "I think you need all your friends about now. Can you afford to risk disruption?" He was bluffing like mad. "Is your secret so deadly when I already know so much?"

Bayes hesitated. The argument was weak enough, yet it did appear to carry some weight with Bayes, who suddenly braced himself, sighing heavily, and said: "All right. It amounts to this,

Brown. When we were passing through this part of Kansas, up from the Oklahoma crossing, we were accosted by a party of — "

The ex-captain broke off abruptly, looking up and round as a young woman's voice shouted: "Stay where you are, you sidewinders, and keep your hands away from your shooting irons! We're coming in right now, and we'll gun you all down if even one of you makes a false move!"

Brown stood there blinking. He had supposed that he and the rest of the Rocking R crew had at least thirty square miles of the surrounding countryside to themselves, but now figures were emerging from the trees and the ground on all sides of the encamped drovers, and he guessed there would be thirty guns at the ready.

A Rocking R man stirred in the firelight — perhaps not belligerently at all — and a gun banged and down he went.

"No!" Colonel Riches bawled. "No

more of that! You've heard what's what! I don't want anybody else hurt!"

"That was wise of you, Colonel Riches," declared the woman who had voiced the earlier cautionary words, revealed now at the other side of the campfire as a tall and shapely blonde, who was dressed in buckskin riding gear and held her rifle as if she knew how to use it — "and just in time. I said you'd be shot if you gave cause, and so you will be. But we want to keep you alive a little longer yet, because a whole flock of lynchings will suit us a lot better."

"I don't think you know what you're saying, woman!" Riches gasped. "You mean to hang us?"

"It would be more accurate to say, string you up."

Riches swallowed visibly and blanched a trifle. "Who are you?"

Brown whistled to himself. The colonel might not know her, but he had recognised the blonde the instant that he set eyes on her. Brown had met her about five years ago, down in Oklahoma and close to Elk City, where her daddy had owned the Big B ranch and he had worked the spring round-up to put a little much-needed money into his poke. She was Oriel Beerbohm, her father's only child and perhaps the prettiest girl in the Middle West. Yes, her curves were even better than he recalled, her hair had a richer light upon it than summer corn, and the perfect face under her flat-topped plains hat was no less intelligent than lovely. But her eyes chilled him now. A brilliant blue by daylight, they had once been full of passion and mischief, but tonight they appeared icy and merciless. Oriel had clearly undergone some sobering and maturing experiences since he had last pleasured her — and he didn't like what he saw — but his body still stirred to his memories of her, there in the hay loft, and he wanted her all over again. She was the girl he would and should have married.

Meantime the girl had given Riches her name; and now she added: "Understand this, Colonel, what's just begun here can only end the one way. There'll be no pleas of mitigation and no attempts at negotiation. Tonight you die — all of you! But first we want the truth of what happened to those people of ours who stopped you short of Hellsgate. There are two ways of getting that. Either you tell it simply and straight — or we beat it out of you, cruelly and with delight. What's it to be, Colonel? Will you co-operate — or must we turn brutal?"

"What are you talking about, Miss Beerbohm?" Riches begged, looking utterly bewildered. "I feel you must have received some very false information concerning me and mine. We are just everyday cowmen — working men from Texas — and we are on our way home after delivering a herd of cattle at the railhead in Hellsgate."

"I think all that's substantially true," Oriel Beerbohm said; "but only as far as it goes — and that's nothing like far enough. No, sir! We know for sure that it was your herd our team of cutters rode out to intercept. Those men, experts all, were led by my father, Heinrich Beerbohm, and they haven't been seen or heard of in a fortnight. I'm convinced my father and his friends are dead, and that you and yours murdered them. What did you do with the bodies? Where are those poor souls lying now? Ten good men of this territory — mostly with dependents. Come now, let's have no more lies. Just give us a true account of what happened between you and the herd-cutters, and the rest will be that much easier."

"I'd gladly give you an account if I could, Miss Beerbohm," Riches said glibly. "But I'm still at a loss. We never met your herd-cutters. I could swear that on a pile of Bibles. Presumably we have been accused of picking up cows on our drive up country. Not so! We are most careful, when driving a herd, to avoid picking up strays and such en route. Everybody who knows the Rocking R drovers will tell you that."

"Everybody who knows you says exactly the opposite!" Oriel Beerbohm retorted. "You've been in trouble before about the number of local cows that your passing herds have sucked in. You're richer by thousands of dollars through your stealing."

"I'd ask you to be careful, Miss Beerbohm," Riches said, his manner changing from the ingratiating to the stern. "We have lists and tally checks to counter these allegations."

"You're caught," the girl reminded the colonel disdainfully. "We're not listening to anything you want to tell us — except what we wish to know. I've told you what that is, and I advise you to speak up. It may encourage you to know, sir, that we have a full-blooded Apache with us. He's an expert on burning bellies with firebrands and breaking fingers and toes — and he enjoys putting out eyes. Will you be the first to test his skills, Colonel Riches?"

"Enough of this, girl!" Riches counselled, his manner hardening. "You're bluffing! It takes a lot more guts than you have to employ Indian torture!"

"Is that so?" Oriel Beerbohm mused, suddenly tilting the muzzle of her rifle and pressing the trigger.

The colonel yelled with pain, grabbing at his torn left ear; but he had hardly touched the first injury, when the girl's Winchester went off again and ruined his right ear in the same fashion. "How does white girl's torture suit you then?"

"You bitch!"

"Then don't force me to convince you further," the girl warned. "I'm a hard woman, Colonel, and you've plenty of soft parts. Including private ones." Both shocked and amused, Brown drew air deeply into his lungs and had the feeling that this had gone about far enough. Oriel was beginning to sound devilish — a creature lost to all reason and decency — and he could not allow her to become that. Perhaps he could halt her reckless progress into the depths of human foulness before it went too far. As he saw it, her soul was more important than her grievances, awful though they might be. This girl, who had once been full of love, was now half eaten up by hatred. Maybe a reminder of warmer and kinder times would help tilt her back to what she had been before. Dammit, they had billed and cooed together, hadn't they, and it had all been gentle and indescribably good? He couldn't let her go to hell on Riches's account; the skunk was not worthy of it. "Oriel!" he shouted. "You mind your tongue, my woman! Your pa would take his boot to your bustle if he could hear you now! What the heck are you doing to yourself? Have you gone clear off your rocker?"

The blonde looked up sharply, peering into the gloom beyond the fire with a concentrated gaze. "What?" she demanded tightly. "Who is that?"

"It's me, Orie — Jack!"

"Jack Brown?"

"The same."

"That's all we need!" the girl cried, her face advancing as she peered even more deeply into the pool of shadow which obscured Brown and George Bayes. "It's the big sneak himself! Jack, it is you, you polecat!"

"Sounds like I'm doing fine," he mourned.

"You said you'd come back!"

"Sure did," he admitted. "But I didn't say when. Fact is, I didn't get anywhere near Elk City again."

"We've moved anyhow."

"Suspected so," Brown returned. "Elk City is hundreds of miles away. Where are you now?"

"Near Evergreen. We moved up this way last year. Dad needed more grass."

"Cattlemen are like that."

"Jack, I want to speak with you — privately."

"Before you string me up with the rest?"

"You need hanging as much as any of them!"

"Sounds like I'm out of favour," he remarked. "Okay, if you want to bend my ear some, let's get on with it."

The girl jerked the barrel of her Winchester towards the timber at her back. "In the trees. You're not going to like this!"

Brown already sensed that. That he had offended the blonde he was well aware, and retribution was due. But the way Orie was now, she'd as lief kill him as look at him.

6

His chin upon his collar stud, Brown slouched past the campfire and into the timber. He heard Oriel Beerbohn giving a series of rapid commands behind him. It seemed that she was the actual leader of the men who had appeared from the night, and she called on two individuals, Daniel Ferguson and Donald Foster, to take over while she was away. They were to obey her main order before all else, and it was that Colonel Riches and his drovers should be disarmed and then bound at the wrists ready for hanging. There was a grim finality in the air, and Brown realized that the girl had meant every word that she had spoken before and was at the end of both her probing and patience. The lynchings would take place, and the revelation of his presence had probably done no more than make matters worse.

He halted under a birch tree. Oriel Beerbohm strode up behind him within the minute. She boxed his ears for him at once, letting fly with both front and backhanders. Brown crouched away from her, trying to protect himself with hunched shoulders and upraised arms. "Will you cut it out, Orie?" he asked through his teeth. "You're beginning to hurt!"

"That was the idea!" Orie assured him, sounding vinegary enough for forty. "You are a stinker! And to get yourself mixed up with that bunch of murdering crooks! Or have you been playing it smart? Does that man Riches have a lead on the fellow you once told me you were hunting down to avenge your brother's death?"

"Hasher?" Brown queried. "He's dead, Orie, as of two days ago, but not by my hand." He went on to tell her as briefly as possible of how the consumptive ex-sergeant had died in Goodman's saloon, ending: "The Rocking R is just a job, but I'm wondering if that bushwhacker who got Hasher may be in the company. There's got to be more to it than meets the eye, and I've been asking myself what. Clyde Riches has covered a fair piece of ground in his time."

"Well, I'm glad you didn't kill Hasher, Jack," the blonde said in a voice which was much closer to the one that he remembered as hers. "I'm glad you're over that vengeance thing. It was ruining your life."

"Yes. But I don't seem to have settled much."

"We have to let the dead bury the dead."

"Listen to who's talking!" he mocked.

"This is different," the girl said shortly. "It's recent, and there's justice involved. For a lot of people."

"I wish you were back down Elk City way."

"Yes, it was a good life."

"And you were the best thing about it, Orie. We sure had us a whale of a time!"

Again her hand struck out.

"Ouch!" he complained. "What was that for?"

"Because I'm not like that, Jack. I don't want to be a dirty memory."

"Come on!" he protested, rubbing his cheek. "I wasn't the first, Orie, and don't tell me you didn't enjoy it as much as I did. What's the good having regrets?"

"I've none for me."

"Well, it's a sure moral you've none for me!" Brown scoffed.

"No, they're all for a little girl I've left at home. Your daughter."

Brown's jaw almost hit his boots. "Oriel," he said, and he had never meant the words more deeply in his life, "I'm sorry. How did it happen?"

"You have the cheek to ask that?" the girl asked, her young face flaring with the intensity of her feelings. "Didn't the other little boys tell you what happens when you plough the field and scatter? Really, Jack!"

"It's a facer all right," Brown confessed. "Just goes to prove — " He shrugged, since it was no good going on with that. "What's the child like?"

"More like me than you — mercifully," Oriel Beerbohm responded. "But she's got your wicked eye and scheming ways."

"Poor little thing."

"Poor little thing — nothing!" the blonde scorned. "Her grandfather has spoiled her hopelessly, and she's got the rest of us wound round her little finger. I wonder where she got that from?"

"Can't think."

"No? Well don't come near Evergreen. You're liable to get into serious trouble if you do."

"You're going to string me up," he reminded. "All my earthly troubles will be over."

"Don't be such a fool!" the girl protested. "I'm not likely to hang my daughter's father. Especially as I knew from the first that you hadn't come up from Texas with the Rocking R cowboys. Names had been named, by people who had met the Riches herd, and yours would have been among them." She fell silent for a moment, then added, as if under some kind of compulsion: "I wish you had been. You'd never have let happen what I believe did happen."

"Of that you can be sure," Brown said emphatically. "I'm not much good, but I'm no crook or killer either." He let go a deep sigh. "So old Heinrich's missing?"

"He's dead, Jack," the girl said flatly. "I feel it in my heart. Him and the rest of them. We sent the Parker boys into Hellsgate last night to throw a scare into Colonel Riches and his men. They had been told to accuse the colonel of murdering our herd-cutters and hiding the bodies. It worked just as we hoped it would and got Riches and company on the run. We've been shadowing the sorry bunch for hours. Now we've got them where we want them."

"What about Sheriff Lotus?"

"He'd be way out of his jurisdiction here," Orie Beerbohm replied. "That's part of what we wanted. Range justice beats the court's justice every time."

"Range justice is rough justice," Brown reminded rather sententiously. "It can get you into every kind of trouble, Orie. I know how you must feel about your pa, but you've a small girl to think of too. Have you thought of that?"

"Of course I have."

"Sounds to me like not enough."

"Don't you start trying to interfere in my life, Jack Brown!" she cried angrily. "You've done enough harm!"

"Yes," he admitted humbly. "That's why I don't want to see you come to anything worse."

"I'll take my chances," the blonde said evenly. "Now I'm giving you yours. Get on your horse and ride — and I'll hope never to see you again."

"Okay, Orie," Brown responded.

"But I'd surely like to see the child."

"Esther is mine, Jack," Orie cautioned. "Visit the Big B, mister, and whether it's me in charge or my father, the dogs will be set on you. If you survive that, you'll get a horsewhipping. And if you should even then persist — "

"Hang me now."

"Please, Jack!"

Brown nodded. He was not going to make it tougher for her than it had to be. It took two to make a bargain, but it was invariably the woman who paid. "Thank you, Orie," he said, "and goodbye." Then he turned away and walked back out of the trees, with the girl moving at his heels, and he crossed the campsite — at Orie's shout of safe conduct — and headed for where he had left his horse, all too conscious of the loose line and knots of Rocking R prisoners, who had been bound as Orie had commanded and were now standing silently under the gun.

Reaching his mount, Brown stood beside it and threw a quick glance back at the shadowy ground, with its contracting rose of fire, which he had just traversed. While he had no pity for Clyde Riches and company, he did have some conscience and a feeling of responsibility for what was happening. If the members of the Rocking R crew were lynched, it would be a major crime and Oriel Beerbohm would not be able to escape her primary part in the matter. She could go to jail for life, if nothing worse, then what would happen to the child of whose existence he had not dreamed an hour ago? Again, however, there was nothing he could do here, and there would even be a sort of ingratitude involved if he tried. No, he had better go — and leave this awful business to work itself out as Fate intended.

Brown lifted into his saddle, touched right rein, and stirred his horse with a rowel. He edged out into a slot of the blackest shadow away from the moon. Then he heard a voice hiss out his name and drew in again, knowing that it was 'Big Roger' Clunes who was seeking to stay him and that the other — who now occupied the last position in the nearby Rocking R line and was thus the man least visible to his captors — was filled with terror and literally pleading for an ear. "What?" Brown responded, aiming the gruff whisper of his voice downwards.

"That vixen is going to kill us, man," Clunes breathed.

"Could be you all deserve it."

"Mayhap — but don't nobody deserve to be lynched."

The pity was, Brown utterly agreed with him. The lynch rope had no sanction where civilised folk gathered. Yet he shook his head as his thoughts traced back to where they had registered before. If he allowed himself to do something crazy now, he would almost certainly have to pay dearly for it. The men with Oriel Beerbohm would hardly allow him to be spared a second time. Whatever his earlier innocence, they would see any act to save Riches and his drovers as treachery. No, he could not perform a miracle here and must live for himself. "So long, Roger."

"No."

"Yes."

"Jack!"

"Go to hell!"

"Help us out of this, Jack, and I'll — "

"You'll what?"

"I'll tell you what really happened in camp that night at the end of the war when your brother got shot and that Yankee gold got stole away from the firelight."

Brown stiffened. He could hardly credit his ears. The one offer had just been made that he knew himself unable to refuse. He had been thinking of miracles a moment ago and here was one. This was most likely the only chance that he would ever have of setting his mind at rest over Frank's death and that blamed Yankee payroll. He feared that the great risk presented here might prove a destroyer, but he'd simply got to take it. Right — wrong — responsibility — conscience: to blazes with them all! He might owe Riches and the Rocking R men nothing — not even a theoretical civil right — but Frank still had a moral claim on him and he also owed himself something for seven wasted years. "Wait," he murmured tensely; then eased his horse forward again and brought it to the left and round the side of a nearby mound, halting once more and dismounting with the least noise of saddle and foot that he could manage.

Now Brown turned away from the animal and catfooted back to where 'Big Roger' Clunes was still standing as before, with hands tied behind his back and face to the front. Sinking almost to his knees, he put a hand into a trouser-pocket and brought out a large Cavalry shut-knife. Steadying himself precisely in the big man's shadow, he opened the main blade of his shut-knife — which he kept almost sharp enough to shave with — and, lifting the edge with care, slipped it behind the bonds which held Clunes's wrists together and began gently sawing at the constraining hemp, whispering as he did so: "I want you to take this knife, when I've finished freeing you, and go to the next man in line and cut him free too. He can do the same thing for the next man — and so on. Have you got it?"

"Got it," Clunes said, as his rescuer abruptly increased pressure on the cutting edge and the bonds parted. "Gimme the knife."

Brown put the shut-knife in the other's grasp. "When you've freed the next man, creep along and fetch your horse, then join me. We sneak off together."

"Oughtn't we to stick around and see this through?"

"No, sirree!" Brown gritted in reply. "You owe me, mister, and I want my pay. Our talk has to be a very private one. We both know there'll be no talk if there's a mass escape and a fight."

"You don't trust me?"

Trust him? Sooner trust a rattlesnake! "Get on with it, blast you!"

Clunes went creeping away to his right. Brown watched with breath in check. This thing ought to have folded moments ago. It was too exposed and blatant. There had to be a reason why the activity had not been spotted. Then Brown saw that a discussion of some kind was taking place, between Oriel Beerbohm and some of her followers, at the edge of the nearby trees. The eyes of the remaining members of the party were largely upon the speakers. What was in question there? Maybe the talkers were discussing the strength of the boughs in their vicinity. You needed a good strong branch from which to suspend a two-hundred pound man.

Now Brown perceived that Clunes had done his work. It was that hard-natured ex-corporal, Abel Tyson, who had been cut loose. Tyson was just the man to carry on with the knife. Brown doubted that there was a more resolute character around. In pursuit of the present ends, Tyson could be relied upon to forward any risk. Then the man was on his way, and the giant Clunes was moving to the right on tiptoe.

Keeping low, Brown retreated on his horse. There was cold sweat at his temples as he rejoined the animal. The silence yonder was still holding and the knife presumably at work. It seemed amazing, and Brown could feel the tension tightening his throat and trembling in his fingertips. It had been a lunatic venture, yet it was going to succeed. Maybe this was his lucky hour. Even that rat Clunes was acting on cue. But he must not congratulate himself too prematurely, for they had still to complete the getaway.

Brown led his horse to the back of the small mound that covered him. He glimpsed Clunes moving stealthily a few yards beyond him. The other saw him too and, as if by tacit agreement, they lifted into their saddles and jogged slowly northwards — gathering speed and going for it hard when bedlam broke out at their backs and a gunshot rang, more detonations following as the yelling of voices rose to fever pitch and horses began neighing shrilly. It sounded as if a pretty good fight had commenced behind them, but it was no worry of theirs, for the escapers were clear and away.

Ahead of them the north reached high and black, with the Pole Star in view but a shadow of moonshine dimming the constellations there, and they hammered at the earth with the determination of their flight for a full two miles before easing back out of respect for a pair of flagging horses that had already had a very hard day. Now they trotted upwind across the glimmering pastures of a cool midnight, and the horses coughed and the riders eased their muscles, looking round at each other as they relaxed and listened

109

at the moonlit shapes of land and sky that filled their wake. "What d'you think?" Clunes inquired.

"God knows!" Brown replied tersely. "Somebody got hurt, that's for sure. But I reckon we're safe enough for now, however it came out."

"Where to?"

"Just keep riding ahead," Brown advised. "You've got some talking to do."

"About what?"

"Just spill it. You know about what."

"I lied," Clunes said. "I've nothing to tell. I had to get your help somehow."

"Don't give me that, Roger!" Brown warned. "You were on the verge of fouling your trousers, man. The truth was all you knew in that minute. A lie would have strangled you!"

"You're blowing it too big," Clunes persisted. "That bitch had let you go. I was cashing in on it — for all the boys. Weren't that just natural?"

"You're a cheat!"

"I was just a guy doing what he

had to do, Brown," the big man contradicted. "You were the one out for all you could get."

"I trusted you."

"More fool you then!" Clunes sneered. "The rest are my excuse."

"You stinking hypocrite!" Brown yelled, a bombshell bursting in his head, and the great red flash carried him out of his saddle in a tremendous spring and he met Clunes firmly, chest to shoulder, and carried him out of his seat and brought him crashing to the ground, where the impact separated them and sent them rolling apart.

Though dazed by the impact, Brown was the first of the pair to his feet. There was light enough to see by and, as Clunes's head rose towards him a moment later, he also struck first, hooking with left and right; but, though the blows were plenty hard enough to have stretched most men senseless, the giant simply spat and flapped his way through them, wobbling fully erect and shoving his lighter opponent off balance with a long left arm while mouthing horrible threats.

Steadying up, Brown returned to the attack. Ducking through Clunes's guard, he belaboured his man about the body, then switched to the giant's head again, blood and teeth flying as he hammered at nose and mouth. Clunes swore, giving ground now, and once more Brown's fists thudded into the other's solar plexus and meaty sides, deliberately ending up with a barrage of blows that went very low indeed and had his adversary shrieking with agony. Then he kicked Clunes in the right knee, frankly hoping to cripple him, but he misjudged his effort and the toe of his boot only skidded off the side of the big man's leg. Not that it mattered much, for Clunes was already doubled up and past defending himself, and Brown had to do no more than steady himself again and hit the other at will, his blows crunching against jaw and temples until Clunes could take no more and finally flopped backwards onto his shoulder-blades, where he lay moaning to himself and clutching at his lower body.

But Brown hadn't done with the big varmint yet. Still beside himself with fury, he leapt astride the spreadeagled giant and seized him by the throat, digging in his thumbs and summoning every ounce of his strength as he started to throttle Clunes and soon brought him to the point where his eyes were staring wide in horror and his limbs were jerking and flapping like featherless wings. Now the big man sobbed, gurgled and dribbled, and it was obvious that his senses were leaving him and might never return; so, getting a hold on himself, Brown eased the grip of his hands a little and allowed his enemy to get some air into his starved lungs with a single shuddering gasp. Then he restored the force of his grasp to much what it had been before, letting Clunes begin to suffer badly again before saying: "I swear to God you're a dead man, Roger, unless you give me a true account of what happened that night!" For the second time he eased his grip on the giant's throat. "This is your one and only chance, mister! If you don't talk, I'm going to close my hands again and hold on until you're dead! So what's it to be?"

"Have — have a little — little mercy, Jack!" Clunes pleaded squeakily.

"None!" Brown responded implacably, and he began to force his thumbs into his enemy's windpipe again.

7

Brown felt 'Big Roger' go completely limp beneath his weight; then, using what was undoubtedly the last vestige of his breath, Clunes piped out: "Kay."

Though instantly releasing his grip on Clunes's neck entirely, Brown kept his hands in place and let his touch itself remind his enemy that the threat to his life had not gone away. "Good," he said. "Start talking."

The big man's upper body pumped and made strange noises, and he was clearly in a bad state of distress as he croaked: "Love o' heaven, Jack, a moment — a moment!"

Lifting himself off Clunes's torso, Brown settled back on his knees, giving the other's lungs freedom to expand. The moment of respite was provided, and then several more — but only in the cause of expediency — for you could hardly expect a guy who had been more than three-quarters strangled to be immediately fluent with words when ordered to speak. All the same, Brown gave Clunes a hard nudge in the ribs when he thought the big guy was ready for it.

"It was — the colonel," Clunes said. "Him — him and George Bayes. They called in the men they figured they could trust, then organised it. I saw an' heard everything as Riches's servant.

"It was simple enough. Us faithful just bellied down in the dark behind the colonel's tent and let fly with our Henry repeatin' rifles. Then Carl Judes crep'up and whipped that Yankee gold from beside the campfire. The bullets flyin' about had everybody on the jump and nobody saw a thing. It sure was neat, Jack.

"Riches, y'see, had always had this notion of a ranch in Texas to provide for him and the chosen ones when the war was over, so what could have been more providential than how that payroll just fell into our hands the day it did? The colonel had seen the land he wanted, when we crossed the High Plains in the summer o' Sixty-four, and he reckoned only a pack o' imbeciles would pass up that chance we had. He said it was meant to be, and there weren't no fools in C Troop. You know that, mister."

"I sure do," Brown said, showing his teeth to the moon. "Seven years I spent doggin' that poor bastard Hasher! He was innocent of everything — except of deserting because he believed that the bluecoats would celebrate victory by massacring our boys for fun. I can't blame him for that. Seemed to me it could so happen. Did Clyde Riches have him murdered in Hellsgate as part of putting an end to him, me, and that whole saga of the wartime gold?"

"That was the idea," Clunes admitted. "It's something that keeps blowin' up and reminding folks of things better forgotten. George Bayes said, when all

117

the facts was in, he'd go into town and do the drygulchin's. Fouled up, didn't he? And got wounded too."

"I thought that was the way of it," Brown said heavily. "I could see Bayes was hurt, when I met him in Riches's tent, and it all somehow fitted — though for some reason I can't quite explain now, I couldn't accept it then."

"Ain't easy to believe common wrong of our betters," Clunes observed. "The cap'n was even more keen to see you dead than the colonel was. George Bayes is a worry-gut, and questions have been asked before today, down in the Red River valley, about Colonel Riches and his wealth. 'Cos he didn't have a red cent before the Secession. Folk wonder, and they whisper. They ain't blind or stupid, and you can always depend on jealousy and what it does."

"Yes, anybody who keeps asking about the gold will always be a threat to Riches and Bayes," Brown sighed.

"Their heads will rest uneasy to their dying days."

"Let me up, Jack," Clunes urged. "I've told you what you wanted."

"There's a bit more," Brown said, his mouth tightening again. "I haven't finished with you yet."

"What else?" Clunes demanded, heaving ominously in proof that his strength had returned.

"What else?" Brown queried. "Plenty else. You and the Rocking R bunch murdered those Kansan herd-cutters, didn't you? I want to know the truth about that, and where the bodies lie."

"Look here, Jack," Clunes said harshly, "I'm not confessin' to murder."

Brown still had his revolver. Now he drew it and pressed the muzzle to Clunes's head, thumbing back the hammer. "Yes, you are. And forget fighting me again. I'm no longer in the mood for fisticuffs. I'll blow your brains out if you don't tell me about those killings and where the bodies lie. Come on now, Roger — speak!"

119

"It was going to be them or us!" Clunes protested. "That Heinrich Beerbohm was a feisty old cockerel. We got the sign from Riches to shoot first — 'cos them Kansans was workin' up to it. Sure, we'd picked up some cows here and there, drivin' up from the Red — y'can't help that — but them herd-cutters had called us rustlers and only fit for hanging." His tones once more pleaded for reason. "See how it was, Brown? We was in danger for our lives. What would you have done?"

"Made good and sure they didn't have to call me a rustler in the first place," Brown replied, grinding up the words and spitting them out.

"Can't talk to you reasonably, that's for sure."

"I've listened, Roger," Brown said, implacably as before, "and fairly and squarely. Where did you put those bodies?"

"Jack, you don't want to know."

"Yes, I do."

"It could be a liability, you fool."

"I'll chance that. If I'm on borrowed time, I'll just have to borrow some more." Brown jiggled the hammer of his gun. "Roger, you're just a hairsbreadth from dead!"

"God-damn you, Brown!" Clunes bit in return. "We can't be all that far from the place now. I'd put it just a few miles north of here. There's a hill, high for these parts — real prominent, as you might say — and it's got a ring o'trees around — "

Brown glanced up quickly as Clunes broke off, for shouting voices and drubbing hoofbeats had become audible not far down country from where they lay. It seemed to Brown that he could pick out Colonel Riches's voice among those calling, and he realized that riders yonder could be men now escaping Oriel Beerbohm and her party. It was even possible that the reverse was the fact of it. Either way, Brown had no wish to make contact with any enemies at present riding the prairie nearby — for the scale of danger represented was about the same all round — so, feeling that he must sacrifice, at least for now, the final details that he required from Clunes, he holstered his Colt and let the fellow up, saying: "We shouldn't take any chances of getting run across, mister. Our horses fetched up hard by. Let's hop on them and ride. Eastwards, I think!"

The mounts were cropping under the sky's broad gleaming about forty yards beyond them. Hurrying to the creatures, the two men clambered into their saddles. Brown headed off to the left of the moon, and Clunes went with him. All rumour of the horsemen recently heard soon faded into nothing. Brown rather expected that the big man would stick to him as a matter of policy, and made no new threatening noises as they rode neck-and-neck; but when, presently, they passed into the bank of mist that filled a prairie hollow, the gap between them began to widen and he started to wonder what Clunes had in mind.

After a minute or two, Brown called to his companion — prompting an answer with several repetitions of his low shout — but silence and the vapours about him hung as the same clinging veil and, when he emerged from the mist at the other side of the low, he realized that Clunes had simply done what he might have expected from the first and parted from his elbow at the earliest safe opportunity. Well, he guessed that wasn't much of a loss. The big man had never possessed the makings of a good companion, and he had beaten or scared from the other most of what he had so desperately needed to know concerning the past and the even more pressing present. Clunes could ride tomorrow down — and bad luck to him, the hellion! The night was company enough for an honest man.

Even so Brown felt the loneliness of the plains. The wind keened softly, and the young grass picked up a faint polish as it bent through the moonbeams. His mount's pace fell to a dawdle. The animal needed rest, and so did he. He'd certainly been living at a rate these last twenty-four hours. If great pressure appeared in your affairs, you had to meet and absorb it, but he felt that much of what he had been suffering of late had been his own fault. It had occurred to him, when he had flattened the enormous Clunes, that he wasn't as young as he had once been, and now he was inwardly hoping that others might yet avenge the wrongs of his life for him. Hadn't he put the whole concept of human retribution from him when he had shunned the vision of two graves at Hellsgate? What had happened since then was not that important to him really. Perhaps he ought to forget everything at this minute and give up. He could let the wind take him: just like a carefree thistledown riding a summer breeze. Hatred turned your belly, and he had seen enough of turmoil and blood. Right now he simply wanted to be out of it. If he had also done wrong in his time, surely this was his opportunity to slide clear of the yesterdays that contained his folly? The present could not be so unforgiving as to want to hang on to him. Anyhow, what was he but the tiniest speck on this vast land, and neither chance nor destiny could find him in the night. If they looked for him tomorrow, he'd make sure they didn't find him either. He would be wearing a new face, and the bag that contained his misdeeds would be stuffed in the corner where the rubbish was dumped. He had the power to elude both heaven and hell. He was smart and well up to it.

He smiled ironically into the night. Well, a fellow was allowed to deceive himself sometimes. But how convenient his plan would be. No more responsibility for the past — nothing but a clean white tomorrow. To be that free would be a relief like no other. Yet he began to feel uneasy about himself. Was he becoming a moral coward? The past and future had no umbilical cords. It all counted or nothing did. The very fact of doing forced a man to finish what he had started; for good or ill. He must face up to what threatened to overwhelm him here, and go back to pay for his share of this night's madness. He had betrayed Oriel Beerbohm for his own ends, and now he must return and make it up to her. If she and her friends hanged him, it would only be a little more than he deserved. Where would they be now? He'd find out tomorrow — providing he could elude Colonel Riches in the process.

Fetching his mount round, Brown faced into the west. But then he heard a faint sound and a black shape quivered for a moment atop of ridge off to his left and seemed to drop into nothingness. Brown's scalp crept and his lungs bated. There was somebody moving out yonder. He was being steathily tracked. Hunted even. Then fire streaked at the corner of his eye and a rifle boomed. In the same split instant his horse let out a screeching neigh and climbed to the vertical, pitching him out of the saddle and into heavy contact with the ground. He lay there with a frightful pulsing in his brain, and his senses ebbed and flowed. He was just short of losing consciousness.

Now he fought to regain the full power of his wits and at least something of his mobility. It had to be Roger Clunes threatening him from the grass, and the big man was going to kill him unless he could get in first. Moving the little that he could, he drew his gun again and cocked it, letting the Colt rest across his thigh as he waited for his would-be killer to close in. What a noodle he had been! He should have expected this to happen from the moment that Clunes had left his side. The other had been bound to try to kill him, for Clunes had told him Colonel Riches's secrets — and Clunes lived in terror of the colonel and would have foreseen his own death if he couldn't silence Brown and thereby make matters right. Ascribing godlike powers to his boss, the giant would have felt totally obliged to compass Brown's murder with his saddlegun, since he would have apprehended no other way out. It was too obvious for words, and the only hopeful thing about it was, that having seen his intended victim tumble to the earth, he would assume that his bullet had found its target. If Clunes should prove careful in his almost certain approach, and stand off for a second shot, this thing could still be touch-and-go. Yet, through it all, Brown did not really want to slay the man, for the giant still had bits of information that he needed. This business was suddenly more complex than it seemed, yet he, Brown, must not make the vital error and do something to invite that early bullet.

Any small doubts as to Clunes's oncoming were soon ended. Before long Brown felt the tiniest trembling of the earth under the big man's feet. The quiet approach continued, dragging like the slowest of slow marches and, feeling more himself again, Brown kept the fingers of his right hand near the pistol balanced on his thigh. He was ready to make his grab and fire — but only if circumstances didn't allow him to intimidate the other with a sharp command. If he had to shoot, it would be to kill. There was a limit to what he was prepared to risk.

Suddenly Brown was aware of 'Big Roger' looming on his left. Clunes paused, but no sudden bullet came from his rifle. Indeed, surprisingly enough, the weapon wasn't even cocked, as Brown realized when he heard the long gun's breech mechanism sliding as it lifted a cartridge under the hammer. He sucked air; it had to be now. And then, pistol coming to hand, he raised up and tipped onto his left elbow, bracing there with his Colt held steady as he snapped: "No, Roger!"

The man with the rifle jerked backwards in surprise, grunting. Then he pressed the trigger of his weapon, and Brown's revolver echoed the rifle's boom. Clunes's bullet went into the ground just short of its target, but Brown's caught the big man in the body and sent him sprawling onto his back. The downed figure snatched up a leg and kicked convulsively, shuddering into stillness then, and Brown had seen the signs so many times before that he had little doubt the other's life had ended. But, rising, he walked over and examined the giant briefly, confirming that death had occurred. After that he stood above Clunes, feeling a pang of regret — not so much for his enemy's demise as the fact that he had been forced to take a life again. Yet he had given Clunes what chance he could, and every man had the right to defend himself. "Big Roger' had been a southerner and a cavalryman of sorts, but he had also been pure skunk.

Brown palmed his gun away. He knew that for him the night was a little safer now. But the sound of the recent shots had carried, and the noise might just bring somebody to this spot, which meant that it could be foolish to hang about: so Brown located his horse again — no difficult task — and remounted, riding once more towards the Pole Star and suffering a reaction to his latest nervous tension almost at once. He shook in his limbs and felt cold all through; and his fatigue was twice what it had been before. He would find a sheltered spot and rest. There was nothing he could do until sunup anyhow.

Not long after that the moon showed him a broken place in the prairie's surface and he rode down into it, finding that the slot had a protective wall of earth on the one side and a chalk-face on the other. There was dampness present and the air was a bit dank, but Brown had lain in worse places, so he made a seat for himself in a niche and there settled down, head lolling against moss while his drooping horse excluded all draught, and he remained dozing thus until just after dawn, when he rose stiffly from his earthen retreat and yawned himself as nearly awake as he could, cursing the lack of supplies that left him without coffee or a bite for breakfast. The new day stretched before him, a space to be lived through, and he could only hope that its events would not be too harsh and that the needs of his body would be met. So far they always had been, and that bred a kind of faith; but he felt jaded right now and could not believe in much good among the uncertainties that faced him. He guessed he'd better go and hunt for Oriel Beerbohm and her party — if they still had their being — and that way he would at least see what he would see.

Brown rode up out of the slot, and again he headed northwards, the light yellowing about him and promising warmth later on. The mists of the moonscapes were still present, shifting and thinning, and the shapes of the skyline hardened through them and shrank again, the whole forming an insubstantial ocean of rising land, falling heaven, and a pearly bubble which enclosed all in images that might even be what they seemed. So it was, with glimpses of grazing bison and flying deer, that Brown was beginning to feel that there was no real world to contain his all too mortal bones, when he saw the hill which formed a conical mass to the west of him and seemed somehow familiar — though he was sure that he had never before set eyes on it in his life.

Puzzled by this, he abruptly recalled the now dead Roger Clunes's description of the hill where he had been led to presume that the bodies of the murdered herd-cutters had been hidden away. Now, turning his horse speculatively, Brown rode directly towards the hill, at first believing its summit to be capped with dark stone; but then, on drawing nearer, he saw that the rock was an illusion and that the apex was in fact crowned with an impressive ring of timber, detail which once more related nicely to Clunes's description of the not too distant eminence that Brown had received from him. Indeed, he was pretty certain that he was on track for the hill in question, and he gazed up at it with an excitement that was not unflavoured by apprehension. For the prospect of attempting to ferret out corpses already a week or two old was not at all to his liking.

The light improved, and soon the dark hill filled Brown's vision. He tipped his head back further and further as he viewed its tree-girt summit. Then he reached the base of the cone and began to ascend, finding that part of his business unremarkable enough — for there were no rock-piles or broken places to impede him — and he entered the deep circlet of conifers and harder timbers at a height of about three hundred feet and found himself among clumps of holly, hawthorn, redbud, ferns and other light undergrowth, that were without any game tracks or set paths that led towards the crest of the height. Thus he was compelled to force his own passage, but this again was not all that difficult, and he reached the top a few minutes later and found to his surprise that it held a deep pit which had undoubtedly been a volcanic vent in the far past and was now filled with water and overhung by branches and lined in places by festooning vines. It also provided a rather weird atmosphere, for the liquid in the pit absorbed the colour of the sky and transmuted it into something like the repellent eye of a jungle predator.

Dismounting at the eastern edge of the pit, Brown gazed up and around him — his neck and skin creeping to the oppressive stillness of this isolated summit — and, hunkering down, he took in his surroundings a little at a time. Common sense suggested that the bodies he sought had been cast into the depths below and were now lying at the bottom of the vent itself. Well, there was only one way to ascertain the truth of that: he must swim down into the dark, stagnant-looking waters and confirm his fears by locating some of the corpses.

Jacking himself erect once more, Brown put a hand to his mount's bit and, picking out the best ground cover, began leading the horse off to his right and round the edge of the pit. He walked to the vent's further side, making for a spot where the wall of the hollow had collapsed into a ramplike spread of boulders and dirt — which met the waters of the pool themselves and looked easy enough to scramble up and down — then, after tying his mount behind a dogwood screen, stripped to his long pants and massaged himself all over in preparation for the obvious chill to come.

Then, moving very gingerly, he made his way down the collapsed portion of the vent's wall and came to the edge of the sunken pool, pausing momentarily to gaze down at the wavering image of himself which the black and glassy surface of the pit was mirroring back at him.

Now he dived in, and down he went, arrowing. The water was even colder than he had expected, and he felt chilled to the liver as his plunge took him deeper and deeper into the liquid. The depths were thick and nasty, choked with waterlogged timber and vegetable waste, and he soon found himself wondering if they actually had a bottom, but he reached the floor of the pit at about twenty feet and discovered that he could see around him for a reasonable span, though as through a glass darkly.

He criss-crossed the immediate bottom of the pool for the next fifteen or twenty seconds comfortably enough — for he was blessed with a fine pair of lungs — and might have kept up this limited search for a bit longer, but it was already apparent that there was nothing to find in this part of the vent, so he surfaced and trod water for a minute or so before swimming to the further side of the steeply enclosed waters and turning up his feet in a new and much steeper dive than his first.

The depth at which he found bottom was much the same as before, but the water seemed clearer on this side of the pool. Indeed he could see the wall that most closely contained him now rising vertically clear of the levels of light which undulated through the liquid and rising to its maximum at the spot where he had first looked down from it. This, when the orientation of the hilltop was taken into consideration, had to be the most likely area of the vent into which the bodies would have been thrown, so he swam with his hands brushing the very floor of the pit and his eyes wide and straining.

Mud came smoking up at him, and bubbles passed him too. The taste of the water was sickening, and his stomach felt like a block of ice; but then he had no more time to dwell on his discomforts, for something pale

138

and ghastly came floating at him in a leaden fashion from the deep, deep gloom of a pot in the bottom of the pit and he found himself face to face with a corpse that literally rubbed noses with him as their foreheads met and he almost drowned in his fright while clawing his way back to the surface amidst bursting globules of his own escaping air. Then safe, and relaxing against the incipient cramp, he floated around for several minutes, coughing and gasping and striving to create a calmer state of mind.

At last his courage returned. This had to be done, and the worst of it had been achieved. He made his third dive. Down he went to the bottom, and now he found himself amidst a whole gaggle of floating bodies. They buffeted him, they clawed, and they spun slowly, their blank eyes staring as their mouths grinned. Despite the chill of the water, Brown's hair stood on end, and he eventually fled for the surface filled with the irrational terror of one expecting to have dead hands grab his ankles and hold him under. It was done now. They were all down there. Thank God he could finally swim out of this loathsome pit with a clear conscience.

His swift overarm strokes brought him back to the sprawling shoreline from which he had set out and, floating there, he gave his head a hard shake to get the water out of his ears. Now he blinked. He must be hearing things. But, no! It was not an effect of immersion, and he was not deceived. He had heard voices echoing down to him from the top of the wall opposite him. Hell-and-dammit! He must have been spotted on his way up here and followed to the summit. He ought to have been more careful; but it was no good berating himself for being thick-skulled and remiss at this remove. The neglect had been his, and he must be prepared to pay for it.

But then he heard a woman scream and sensed that his presence in the pit was not the object of the increasingly animated talk and activity on the lip of ground above him.

8

Suddenly it came to Brown that, though those standing above him had not yet detected his shape floating in the pit, it needed only one man to look over the brink and his presence would be spotted immediately; so he lunged back into deep water and settled from view, crossing most of the pool beneath the surface and coming up in the shelter of a mass of overhanging rock — which he had noticed a few minutes ago — towards the foot of the pit's southern wall.

Moving his arms just sufficiently to maintain buoyancy, Brown listened intently to the raised voices of the people gathered on the curve of the brink high to the right of him. Soon odd words were comprehensible to him, and then phrases and whole sentences. He began to build a clear idea of what was happening above — to grasp that it was Oriel Beerbohm whom he had heard scream just now, and to accept that she was the prisoner of Clyde Riches.

"We have most of them here, boys," he heard the colonel say, "and there's nothing for it but to kill them. The water below is deep enough to cover their remains for all time!" He paused just perceptibly, perhaps awaiting comments or reactions — but his flow was not thus hindered — and he went on to add: "Bind the woman's hands and feet. She goes in alive! That will be her punishment for what she intended doing to us! She can drown as we'd have strangled! We'll be kinder to the men and first shoot them through the brain!"

The woman began yelling again, though her cries were defiant rather than fearful, and Brown was deeply shocked by the suffering and wasted courage which the sounds conveyed. Oriel Beerbohm had never lacked guts and, despite her relative youth, it was plain that she had more than steel enough to face an awful death without begging for her life. Brown's heart went out to her, in an unspoken prayer — and he would have fought the lot of them for her if he could — but, trapped down here as he was, there was nothing he could do but grit his teeth and hang on, keeping his mind on a saving miracle.

There was a long silence. Brown wondered if the colonel had relented. The man couldn't be that bad. Yet he had already proved that he was. His murders were savagely cold-blooded and numerous. It would happen. Nothing could save Orie from his unfeeling cruelty. Then there was movement above. Brown saw the woman, bound as the colonel had ordered, swinging back and forth in the grasp of two strong men. Now they let go of her, and her flying shape curved upwards to the peak of trajectory and then began falling like a stone, a last scream tearing itself from her lips a split second before she hit the water and threw up a considerable splash.

Brown reacted almost without thought. If there was to be a miracle here, he would have to perform it himself. He tipped over and drove himself deep, spearing, as nearly as he could, for the spot where the girl hurled down from above had plunged into the pool, and he spotted her almost instantly, settling towards the bottom of the pit in light that was just beginning to thin out. Legs thrusting, he caught her with surprising ease — but here the difficulty began; for, though he managed to check her descent and pass a hand under the bonds that held her wrists together, he could not get her moving upwards and was forced to the conclusion that her lungs had been flattened by the impact at the end of her fall and that she was little better than any other inert and sinking object.

The girl continued settling, if more slowly now, and she went on doing so despite Brown's desperate efforts to reverse her decline. Down they went into the mud and murk on the floor of the pit and, his own lungs getting tighter and tighter, Brown realized that by now Oriel Beerbohm had probably started drowning; but she still surprised him considerably when, in the very instant that her feet touched solid bottom, she used her doubling legs as springs and thrust upwards — thus greatly assisting the lift that he was still trying to supply, and now they began to rise and Brown closed his mind to all suffering and threw everything he had left into an effort that relied more upon the unseen forces of his will than his swimming prowess and they continued their movement towards the light until his head broke surface and he found himself threshing around in a new battle to save the girl by getting her nostrils above water before it was too late.

Brown was by now bemused by lack of oxygen and, having no previous experience to draw upon in a situation like this, he found himself with no clear idea of what to do next as he circled and circled, flailing frantically. There was no sudden inspiration, and he simply kept going instinctively, drifting by the force of his arm, and all at once he collided with the wall of the pit at a spot close to the overhang from beneath which he had started his dive and felt his soles come to rest on a wide underwater ledge that provided his legs with real purchase. Now, pressing down from his hips and thighs, he lifted again, getting in all the power of his arm and lower body, and he produced a surge of buoyancy that fetched Orie's head and shoulders above water while he dragged her feet into a position on the ledge from which she could to some extent support herself.

Fearing that the blonde might be more or less unconscious, Brown peered closely into her face, but she stared back at him dully and coughed hard, smiling faintly as fluid ran from her nostrils and the corners of her mouth. After that Brown drew her further back into the shelter of the wall that covered them, and they both panted and gasped a recovery from their half-drowned state — though he realized that no true advantage had been gained, for what had happened in the pit must have been seen by eyes looking down from above and new efforts could now be expected to finish the girl off and kill him too. Their deaths had been delayed by perhaps minutes only, and that meant further despair and more suffering. It hardly seemed worth it, and Brown shook his head tiredly to himself. Yet while there was life —

His clearing ears picked up the noise of gunfire. For a long moment he supposed that the shooting must be aimed at him and his companion in misfortune. But then he recalled what Colonel Riches had said about killing the male prisoners in his power and took it that the cattlemen in the trees were having their brains blown out. He imagined vaguely that more bodies would be coming this way shortly — but asked himself what the deuce could be happening over all — and then it occurred to him that the character of the firing had the sporadic crackle of fighting rather than the measured banging of an execution. Now he heard voices calling through the detonations and judged that orders were being given, and his mind became more and more lost for a clear picture of what was taking place above. At least the blonde and he were being left alone, and he decided that it could be worth ignoring everything else and giving his full attention to their problems down here.

The greatest service that Brown reckoned he could perform for Oriel Beerbohm just then would be to free her hands and feet. From his earlier knowledge of her, he knew that she could swim at least as well as he and, if he were able to untie her limbs, he was confident that she would still prove in a good enough state to fend for herself. So, with his fingers chilled to the point of fumbling, he turned the girl's body round and held her against him while he plucked and tugged at the knots which secured her wrists, and he was relieved when he found that they had been loosely tied and yielded to his efforts immediately. In fact he freed her hands within the minute and was able to sink at once towards her heels and, keeping his upturned face just above water, deal with her ankles in the same fashion as he had dealt with her higher placed bonds. Soon she was entirely loose and treading water as ably as he had hoped. Then, pulling at her shirt and pointing, he glided off their underwater perch and made for the brief stretch of the shore beneath the ramp-like collapse in the western wall of the pit. The blonde pursued him without any further prompting, and she easily kept pace with his rapid strokes. They arrived at their landing spot without faltering and both stronger than when they had started.

Scrambling out of the water, Brown turned to offer the girl help, but she didn't need any and crabbed away promptly over the debris at the base of the ascent before them. Now they climbed rapidly away from the waters of the pit and soon gained the ground above, Brown both amazed and puzzled as to how they had been allowed to do this without any form of attack from the land held by their foes at the further edge of the pit, and he thrust out a hand to check his companion as she showed every sign of making for the trees across the way in defiance of the danger that he was convinced must still be waiting there when she ought to have remained in full flight. "What the heck are you about, Oriel?" he demanded. "Do you want to get caught and thrown in again?"

The girl didn't answer, and glancing round, Brown saw why not. A bulky, heavy-featured man, with a greying mutton-chop beard and a livid scar which ran obliquely from right to left across his low, weathered forehead, was lumbering towards them around the top of the pit on their left. Beyond him, on the eastern half of the hilltop, a number of men had gathered under the trees, and it was obvious from the delight registering on every face that all were friendly. "Are you all right, Oriel?" the fleshy man panted, coming right up to the blonde before halting. "I had you figured for dead."

"So did I," the blonde admitted, squeezing water out of her shirt and hair. "I'm okay, Mr Ferguson. All I need is a change. I have some dry clothing in my saddlebags."

"You also have a guardian angel, my girl."

"Yes, though I've called him a few other things before today," the girl returned sardonically. "He cuts a figure of sorts in his long underwear, doesn't he?"

"Oh, don't mind her, Mr Ferguson," Brown advised. "She's as ornery as they come."

"Didn't you tell me last night that he worked for you once, Oriel?" Ferguson asked.

"He works well enough," the blonde acknowledged. "But he brays a lot too."

"There's gratitude for you!" Brown sighed.

"Get some clothes on, Jack," the girl ordered. "You make the place look untidy."

Brown pulled a jib. "Sure, I'll go and put my duds on. Then I'll want to ask what brought about what seems this quite incredible change here."

"I'll be asking the same thing," the blonde said. "And Jack. I know you're a dirty sneak, but don't you go trying to make a bolt for it. We wouldn't like that."

"I'm not going to high-tail it," Brown said, hooking a thumb towards the patch of dogwood and briars that concealed his horse. "My things are over there."

"You're not threatened, mister," Ferguson assured him. "Get dressed, then, and join us over yonder."

They parted, Ferguson and the girl moving to the left and round the rim of the pit, while Brown padded gingerly to the back of the thicket. Here he stripped off his sodden underthings and stuffed them away, putting on his dry outer garments without the benefit of fresh clothing underneath. Then, grimacing as canvas and raw cotton chafed his naked skin, he led his horse out and over the ground which Oriel and Mr Ferguson had recently covered, joining the people who now stood beside their horses under the trees beyond. "Okay," he prompted.

"No," Ferguson said flatly. "We've just done some jawing. You talk first. How did you come to be here? What had you in mind while we were following you on to this hill?"

"Please, Jack," Oriel insisted.

Shrugging, Brown told them what they wished to know with all speed. He put no gloss on Clunes's death or how he had obtained his information from the man, and also spoke bluntly of how his swim to the bottom of the pit had indeed taken him among the bodies of the vanished herd-cutters.

"Did you — find my father?" the blonde inquired tentatively.

Now that was a difficult question to which Brown could not give a completely honest answer, so he said: "It's hard to be sure who you're looking at in all that mud. You should know that. I expect you'll find your pa when we get all the bodies up. That's going to be some job."

"But we'll have to do it," Oriel Beerbohm said sorrowfully. "Thank you, Jack. I can see what you've done — and I know it was the best you could."

He nodded. "This is no easy affair, Orie. I wouldn't swear as to who has

155

truly clean hands. "A pox on that!" Ferguson snorted, from where he was listening not two yards away, and his voice was hard and his expression the same. "We'll net those devils yet. It's a matter of principle first. The rules have to be kept and the wicked punished."

"It appears everybody here feels the same about that," Brown said, looking about him with a careful eye.

Affirmative growls came at him from all directions, and he was not aware of being liked, but he understood that these men had already given up something and come far. They were animated by the desire for a justice that could be seen to be done, and that was as old as the Old Testament itself. "I reckon we'd better be getting on then," he said. "I've no right to hold you all up with my curiosity."

"You're durn tootin'," a hardbitten son of Kansas agreed, squirting tobacco juice through his stained front teeth. "I'd string you up right now. We lost a man in that fight with Clyde Riches, and I figure that was down to you!"

"Ease off, Seth," Ferguson advised. "There's plenty here that I don't like, but this man ain't altogether wrong when you get right down to it. We had a mass lynching in view. Two wrongs don't make a right. Never did."

"I feared you'd lost more than one man," Brown confessed. "What are there — a dozen of you here? I had you rough counted at more than that."

"We split the party after Riches and his men escaped," Orie Beerbohm explained. "Half of us are off searching for the colonel and his murderers somewhere else. A waste perhaps" — her voice tailed off — "but what can you do?"

"Sounds like what happened on this hilltop a while ago was a case of the hunter being hunted."

"Yes," the blonde sighed, "we were intent on catching you, and missed the riders behind us. They took us absolutely by surprise when they came out of the trees at our backs, and it seems that if it hadn't been for the reappearance of the Parker brothers — "

"Weren't we going to get on, Oriel?" Ferguson interrupted. "You can tell him about that as we ride along."

"I can too," Orie acknowledged, mounting up.

Everybody present, including Brown, followed her example, and the bearded Ferguson immediately surged into the lead and headed into the trees on the northern side of the hilltop, Brown feeling constrained to call after him: "Don't you go underestimating Clyde Riches, Ferguson! This is his kind of show. He's a good soldier, I can tell you. Didn't I serve with him long enough? So watch out for the ambushment!"

"Forget it!" Ferguson flung back tersely. "Those guys fled like scared rabbits. They had far places on their minds!"

"As I've heard it," the blonde said, bumping along in her saddle to Brown's right, "they got a bad fright okay. The bullets that Joe and Sammy Parker levered at them out of the bushes winged a man or two and did as much to panic Riches and his followers as their earlier appearance had done to scare us. It was dead lucky those villains imagined the Parker boys a whole bunch of men instead of just two."

"I'll say," Brown agreed, getting the picture of what had occurred to save Oriel's followers from annihilation while he and the girl had been struggling for their lives in the depths of the pool adjacent. "They must have got here behind everybody else just right. I suppose they were riding back down from Hellsgate?"

"That's it," the yellow-haired girl answered. "It could not have been more perfect."

"Nor could it happen so again in a million times," Brown commented, shunning irony. "Makes you start believing there's a God all over again."

"How do you think I felt," the girl asked, drawing her horse wide of the rest and spurring to join Ferguson at the party's head, "when you bore me up as I was sinking through the waters?"

Brown watched her take up position at the forefront. It appeared that Orie had been more deeply affected by her experience in the pit than he had imagined. Well, he had always been aware that there was a very good person inside the inconsequential self that she showed the world; and if he had been able to save her then, it was more than likely that she had helped him since; for he had the feeling that the man named Seth was not the only one of these Kansans who would like to see him strung up. He had been leading a rather charmed life just lately, and could only pray that it would go on.

They moved off the hilltop and cleared the timber about then. Now the ground tilted steeply downwards before them, and Brown had a view of the prairie that reached far into the north. He could see small movements upon the grass close up, in terms of the odd buffalo cluster and a few antelope, but it was the absence of human activity upon it that worried him. While the plains had plenty of hiding places upon their surfaces, he could see nothing within the compass of several miles to conceal a body of horsemen at the gallop, and Colonel Riches and his men ought still to be visible on the panorama of the pastures after leaving this height such a relatively brief while ago. True, the colonel could have led his people sharply to the left and down under the western face of the hill — with the intention of turning into the south presently and once more heading for home — but Brown felt instinctively that this was not how it had been. Heavily threatened as he was, Riches wasn't the type to run away from those who wanted to inflict retribution for his recent crimes. A law unto himself, he had never feared killing those who stood in his way, and Brown was certain that, once the man had perceived his mistake on the hilltop, he would take the most drastic measures to put things right. Murder was the only sure way of removing those who dogged your tracks, and it was the colonel's favourite answer to all his problems. So it would be out of character for him to try using any other method of clearing up the mess he was in here. Brown was more than ever sure that Riches would draw them into a trap — and soon. If only Ferguson and Orie would show some receptivity to the caution that he had so recently urged. Hot damn! He could feel trouble coming again! Why couldn't they?

The riders reached the bottom of the hill. Now, with reins lashing, they headed out into the northern grass. There was plenty of purpose in the set of every torso. Brown was a great believer in self-confidence, and these men had it in Spades, but he would have been even more impressed if they had taken their hilltop lesson to heart and kept a better watch on the land around them than they were presently keeping. But if his companions were subconsciously convinced that their qualities were a magic shield, Brown knew otherwise. He had seen better men than they swept into oblivion by a sudden hail of lead, and he was also a devotee of caution. Thus he rode much of the time raised in his stirrups and sweeping every contour of the plain with narrowed eyes, and he was fully on guard when, moments after believing he had glimpsed the tiniest movement of a man's head amidst the low heave of some tussocks before them, a rattle of shots confirmed the ambush he had feared and Oriel Beerbohm's horse reared in the face of the gunflashes and threw her, while her mount turned completely round and brought Dan Ferguson and another rider down. The shots also told, emptying a fourth saddle, and the incipient chaos in the

Kansan party was already portending panic and a subsequent massacre; so, reacting to his battle experiences and knowing that only men properly led could fight their way out of this, Brown drew his revolver and spurred through to the head of the band, shouting: "Hold together, boys — and charge 'em! They're close packed and tied down in a runnel! We can over-run' em! Come on!"

Brown went in, shooting fast.

9

Feeling the buck of his pistol, Brown kept shifting target as the figures dodged and flattened in front of him. He had little fear of the weapons that spat fire within a few yards of him, but he dared not look back. This was a crazy throw, and almost everything depended on the courage of others. He couldn't do this alone, and if the Kansans failed to back him up he was going to lose — and probably die. His gamble was that most of these men, lifelong horse riders, had fought as cavalrymen — for North or South — in the Civil War, and that they would recognise in his headlong charge a standard cavalry tactic which seldom failed to disconcert ambushers and almost always brought a quick victory in circumstances like the present ones. If the men back there picked up his lead okay, there should be enough of them left in their saddles to put paid to Colonel Riches and his dry-gulching crew. The need was to shoot straight and keep moving swiftly.

Gunsmoke belched and spread, and red flashes were everywhere. Brown felt a bullet tug at the waist of his trousers, and he heard lead spit and hiss as it flew past his ears. An enemy stood up in the natural trench which had been giving him cover. Eyes wild and mouth set, he pointed his rifle into Brown's face, finger squeezing at the trigger. Brown ducked, shooting the other through the chest in the same moment. The shot man toppled backwards, his gun blazing high, and three other figures rose to take his place, all firing at once, but too many cooks spoiled the broth and Brown survived the lacing slugs to plug one of the trio as he lifted his mount over the runnel and slashed backwards with his gun barrel to brain a second before his pass ended.

Impetus carried him forward a few yards more. He believed his six-shooter almost empty and wished to heaven that he had his sabre to use on the return. But he yanked his horse round nevertheless and, coming in from the right and parallel with the enemy position, saw that the charge initiated by him had been given weight by everybody capable of it, and that Clyde Riches had already lost most of his following and had no effective control of the men left. He was himself erect and unafraid, and unscrambling his snarled up fighters by hand, but successive waves of gunfire — triggered down into the runnel — had done their job, and the flying hooves of leaping mounts also. Taking aim and attempting to kill Riches for himself, Brown knew that the colonel — who must have been very sure of his ambuscade — was beaten to the point from which he could not recover, and that it was all down to the kind of wild charge which Riches himself would have

167

instigated in reversed circumstances. Indeed, Brown was so elated by the success that he took it as a required payment on his luck when his gun failed to go off and the exasperated Riches, now showing despair, went racing off along the runnel — to a much deeper and wider part of the prairie fissure, where the horses belonging to his people were hidden — shouting: "Save yourselves! Get the hell out! Follow me if you can!"

That did it. Panic flared. Men leaped and scrambled on the floor of the natural trench. One or two actually sprang out of the runnel and pelted along its northern edge, vaulting back down into it when they reached the waiting horses and straddling the nearest saddle as best they could. After that they pounded out along the low, leaving the great furrow where they could and drubbing off in a direction that more or less converged on that which Clyde Riches was following. A couple of the horsemen from the

Kansan party started after the fugitives, but Brown called them back. The chase might get too tight, and the hunters too few. If that should prove the case, those in pursuit could be too easily turned upon and shot down. As Brown saw it for the moment, there was victory enough here. Riches would never again be able to challenge in force, and the probability was that he would now keep running. If he did other than that, he would be a fool and easy to deal with as and when he appeared. For his stalwarts — men like George Bayes, Abel Tyson and Jim Dibber — were among the slain on view, and that left the colonel almost too weak to worry about. Anyway, he could be hunted down in due course and there was too much here that needed attending before any aspect of the future could be looked at.

After passing a slow eye over the area of blood and death, Brown sailed his horse back across the runnel and rode to where the recently unseated

Oriel was now kneeling beside Daniel Ferguson, who was lying on his right side and obviously in considerable pain. "Shot?" he asked, stepping down close to the girl's side and reloading his revolver as he stood there.

"No, it was the fall he took," Orie answered, looking up and round. "I'm afraid his left shoulder is broken. He needs a doctor to set it."

"I doubt there's one to be had closer than Hellsgate," Brown observed. "That must be a ride of close on thirty miles from here."

"Around that," the blonde agreed. "Our party has another dead man too, and one who took a bullet through his leg. He badly needs a doctor also."

At that moment one of the Kansans sitting his horse close by shouted: "Hey — Oriel!"

"What, Jed?" she called back.

"I can see horsemen coming in from the southwest," the man answered. "It looks like Don Foster and the other half of our men."

Oriel Beerbohm stood up. She peered in the direction given. Brown did likewise. He saw a body of riders who were still about a mile away but coming up fast. "It's Don Foster all right," the blonde confirmed, kneeling quickly to attend the injured Ferguson again. "More hands to help with the wounded."

"There aren't so many of those," Brown growled, casting the nearby runnel a rather malignant glance. "Most of Riches's hellions look dead meat to me."

"I wish I didn't still hate them so," the girl confessed, sighing. "It's all very well to hate a foe when he's living, but it's a waste of energy when he's dead."

Little more was said just then, for the greater part of everybody's attention was on the southwest and the approaching riders, who arrived a few minutes later, their horses prancing and tossing as they reined in. They showed expressions that were mainly grim or serious as they gazed down at the scene of the recent battle. "We heard the shooting, Oriel," said the lean, straight-backed leader of the newcomers, a ruddy and rather fierce-faced man, with a neatly clipped moustache and the first signs of ageing in the wrinkling skin around the prominent tendons of his throat. "It looks like you did all right here."

"Clyde Riches ambushed us," Orie Beerbohm returned. "It went wrong for him. But he and a few of his men escaped."

"Has anybody gone after them?"

"No, Don," the blonde replied. "We didn't have the men at the time."

"We've got them now," Foster commented.

"We've got hurt people here," Brown put in. "Our first job is to get them to Hellsgate."

Foster gave Brown a glance that was at once questioning, uncertain, and a mite hostile. "Who might you be, mister? I seem to remember your face. We have a quarrel."

"No, Don!" Oriel Beerbohm urged. "There's a lot here you don't quite understand. Suffice it to say, if it hadn't been for Jack Brown I'd be dead now — and we'd certainly have lost out to Riches and his ambushers."

"I see," Foster said shortly. "The hero now, are we?" He gave his head a small toss that expressed cynicism. "How bad is Dan Ferguson?"

"Bad enough," said the man on the ground through clenched jaws. "My shoulder's busted."

"Badly," the blonde affirmed. "I'll fix the best sort of sling I can — but I wish it wasn't so far to Hellsgate."

"So do I, girl," the hurt man groaned.

"As to that," Foster said slowly, "I think we can do without the journey. There's a farm not so far west of here. We passed it about an hour ago. Chances are the folk there will help out with a bed — and places for the other injured ones too. Then mebbe one of us could ride into Hellsgate for the doctor. It isn't a perfect solution, I know, but I reckon it's as near as we'll get."

"It sounds all right to me," Oriel said. "Unless somebody else has a better idea?"

"How should they?" Brown wondered. "If Ferguson can stand it, we'll get him on his feet and do what we can for him."

Bracing himself visibly, Ferguson signalled that he was ready, and Brown and two other men eased him erect, while he groaned his agony into the front of his shirt. After that cloth was found and a sling fashioned — Ferguson fortifying himself from Foster's hip flask now — and, when all had been done for him that could be done, he was boosted onto his horse and somebody climbed up behind him to make sure that he would ride steady. Then, with the other injured men also seen to and helped astride, the now considerable body of riders present headed out westwards, leaving two of their number to lay out the dead and do whatever else needed doing at the battle site. All the activity at that time was scrappy and held no real interest, but it couldn't be ignored.

They rode under a big sky that fell into purple edges. Once more Brown felt the presence of the miles and the sameness of the prairie. Here, with hooves faintly rumbling, hell and eternity were at one and, as always, Brown sighed and endured; but not for long. With shoulders square and eyes to the front, Foster led them to an area of cultivated land and, at the middle of this, grey-walled and thatched, stood a farmhouse that would have looked as well in Britain as its present setting. A well-worn path bore them towards the farmyard gate and the big shape of an ageing, shrewd-eyed man, floppy-hatted and straw-chewing, who already lounged there, watching their approach, a red dog on one side of him and a shotgun placed nicely to hand against the fence on the other. "Mornin', folks," he greeted as the leaders of the Kansan party reined in just short of his proprietorial leaning place. "Saw you go past before. I heard the guns too. Busy, ain't you?" He looked the authoritative figure of Don Foster up and down. "Law?"

"Not quite," Foster replied.

"You saw some of us before," Oriel Beerbohm said. "We have some badly hurt people with us. Mr Ferguson there has a broken shoulder, and there are gunshot wounds too. The injured need beds, and we'll have to get a doctor to them from Hellsgate. Can you help? Will you help, Mr — ?"

"Whiteman's the name," the other responded. "'Inky' Whiteman. Can I help? Ain't up to me." Turning his jaw across his left shoulder, he shouted: "Hey, ma!"

The back door of the house opened, and into the yard stepped a well-rounded woman with silver grey hair, faded blue eyes, a small nose, and a mouth into which the seams cut deeply at the corners. "I heard you call, 'Inky'," she said.

"The missus," Whiteman proclaimed. "These folk have got hurt people with them, Ethel. Can you find the injured some place to lie?"

The woman wiped her hands in her apron. "Come on into the yard," she called. "You'd better bring your injured indoors. Can't promise more than two beds. The less hurt will have to go into the root shed. That applies to the rest of you, too, if you're going to stick around."

"We'd be obliged," Orie called back through a cupped left hand. "Dan Ferguson is a family friend, and I'd like to be sure all's well with him before making further plans."

Ethel Whiteman waved assent, and her husband opened the gate which gave access to the farmyard. The Kansan party rode into the chicken-scratched space, with Don Foster and Oriel Beerbohm leading, while

Brown — who was feeling rather useless at the moment — brought up the rear.

"I had better begin that ride to Hellsgate," Foster said, when they had all gathered around the hitching post near Whiteman's kitchen door. "I'll be lucky if I have the doctor here by tonight."

"I'll do the riding," Brown volunteered. "These people may need you around, Mr Foster. I have no place here."

"I didn't want the job," Foster confessed. "You do it then. It might make me see you with a friendlier eye."

Brown smiled faintly, shrugging his shoulders. "Any chance of a fresh horse, Mr Whiteman? This one has been hard used of late, and it's a long way."

"You don't have to go gallivantin' off to town to find a medico," the farmer said, patting the red dog's head as he spoke. "There's a doctor across the way — at the railroad construction camp. He's a company sawbones, but the Kansas and Northern will lend him out in an emergency."

"That's fine," Brown said. "How far?"

"Six miles," Whiteman hazarded. "They were laying track due east of here two days ago."

"Even better."

"Beat it then!"

"I'll have to use your name," Brown said, fetching his mount's head round.

"Goes without sayin'," the farmer acknowledged, an eyebrow raised as he sucked on his straw. "Just tell Quintus Tompkins — he's the construction boss — it's the Whiteman farm Doctor Kelling is needed at."

Brown raised a hand in salute, and headed for the farmyard gate. Passing through it, he checked eastpoint against the position of the sun then, riding between Whiteman's cornfields, he regained the open plains and hit up a canter, making his guess now as to the probable position of head-of-steel today. The rails moved on inexorably, and might by this date be two or three miles beyond the point that Whiteman had supposed them to be. Thus a shift of a few degrees to the right seemed in order, and Brown drew his horse that much closer to the sun, hoping that he would cut new track just above the camp that he wished to reach within the next thirty minutes.

The featureless grasses undulated ahead, and Brown was imagining the new cowtown that the Kansas and Northern Railroad meant to connect to their system with this latest ironroad, when he heard a train whistle pretty well dead ahead of him and knew that his rough calculations had placed him more or less exactly on course.

Confident now, he kept riding straight to the front and minutes later he rode down into the wide shallow valley along which the new track lay, and he saw the rust-coloured tents and rough wooden huts of the construction camp itself about a half a mile away to his left.

He could see the smoke of the cooking fires above the place, and there was also a smell to it, while the locomotive that he had heard was panting nearby, flatcars strung out behind it that bore many tons of ties and the new rails themselves. Far to the right, the work at head-of-steel was also visible and, with so much of importance going on, Brown expected to be challenged by an armed guard at any moment.

In the event, he entered the camp — after correcting his course and riding up to it — without being challenged at all, and he had to find somebody for himself among the tents who could tell him where Quintus Tompkins, the construction boss, might be found, and he was directed to the centre of the camp and the largest tent present — a battered affair, with an open front and a pavilioned top that made it look not too dissimilar to a desert potentate's dwelling — where he found the man he was seeking seated at a collapsible table and drawing on a cheroot as he studied what appeared to be a newly sketched map of the district. Large, plump and roundfaced, with a naturally tonsured crown and level but not unkindly eyes, Tompkins looked up abruptly at the approaching Brown and, tapping ash away from his smoke, asked rather crisply: "Is there something I can do for you? If it's a job you want, go and see the foreman."

"A job's the last thing I'm looking for right now," Brown assured the other; and he went on to explain how matters were on the Whiteman farm and that medical help over there was a pressing need. "I'm here to request the services of Doctor Kelling," he concluded.

"Whiteman sent you, eh?" Tompkins considered the matter for a moment, then nodded and said: "Yes, we can spare Kelling for a few hours. There's not much for him to do here at the moment. I daresay he'll be glad of the chance to ride over to the Whiteman farm and treat something more serious than he usually finds his lot with us."

He rose to his feet and stretched, a sweaty, bulging figure, leaving his map where it fell and locking his cheroot firmly into the right-hand corner of his mouth. "Stay here. I'll go and find Kelling myself."

Brown held his ground. He took up a loafer's stance at his mount's shoulder and prepared himself for a wait; but Tompkins reappeared after a minute or so and beside him walked a small, dark man who was carrying a medical bag and had a withdrawn look about him. "This is Doctor Kelling," the manager said by way of introduction.

"Doctor," Brown acknowledged. "I'm Jack Brown."

"I understand you've had some excitement, Brown," the medical man said in a stronger and more decisive voice than Brown had expected.

"That's a way of putting it."

"You can tell me about it as we ride along."

"That I will," Brown promised.

Then Tompkins called to a camp

hand who was loitering nearby. He ordered that a horse be fetched for the doctor. The worker signalled compliance and vanished. Now the trio kicked their heels and spoke disjointedly, waiting for the man to return — which he did after a while, leading a sorrel gelding that was saddled and ready to ride. The camp hand held the mount's head while Doctor Kelling climbed into leather, and Brown swung up at the same time. After that the pair rode out of camp, passing an oak tree and some perimeter sheds on the way, and spurred into the grass beyond, climbing now towards the greater spread of plains beyond the shallow valley in which the railroad ran. Now, prompted by a single word from his companion, Brown told how Ferguson had received his broken shoulder and the other casualties their bullet-wounds, though he kept the history of the events behind the gun battle down to the briefest sketch. Kelling grunted now and again, and nodded a few times, but he made no actual comment on anything Brown said. Indeed, he proved as withdrawn — and even aloof — as Brown's first impression of him had suggested, and, with the account of the fighting done, he lapsed into a state of total silence and rode along without any further interest in his company.

Brown shrugged to himself. Folk were as they were, and you took them as you found them. He, too, could stand the silence; though there was a strange sense of everything hanging fire around him. The violence and threats in which the day had begun had appeared to be over when Clyde Riches and the survivors of his bunch had fled willy-nilly, yet a residue of their hatred lurked behind the smiling noon, and Brown wondered whether he had been guilty of muddled thinking when the firing had stopped. Perhaps he should have cast everything else out of his mind and gone after the colonel for himself. Risk there would have been, yes, and lack of order too, but the one he didn't care about and the other was bound up in responsibilities that were not his. He should have broken away from Oriel Beerbohm and her Kansans and stuck to his own reasons for it all. He had re-engaged his desire to avenge his brother Frank if he had ever truly disavowed it — and killing the man who had caused Frank's death could be the only satisfaction there. Yes, he should have up and galloped after Riches, but he had attached himself to Orie's party now and would have to reconcile himself to the kind of weak reasoning that had put him there. If a man was ever fully conscious of why he did this or that.

Pulling himself out of the reverie that had briefly claimed him, Brown looked up and saw that he was already in sight of the Whiteman farm again. Raising his eyes still further, he slowly circled the skyline with his probing gaze, for he had the feeling that the doctor and he were being observed by a watcher other than one who might be legitimately doing so from the farmyard ahead.

Then, for an instant — it seemed to the uncertain Brown — a rider, straight-backed and firm of line, lifted into a notch between two hillocks on the southern tack, found himself spotted, and sank from view again, a ghost, possibly, of the retina, but Riches himself whether in flesh or illusion, and Brown felt a sickening jolt under the heart. Was the man still there, and plotting anew? Did he never give up? It might be that he could not. Perhaps only the death of all would satisfy him. If that were the truth of it, he had become one of the most dangerous men alive.

10

Brown and the doctor rode into the farmyard about ten minutes later. 'Inky' Whiteman and Oriel Beerbohm came out of the kitchen door to greet them as they dismounted at the hitching post. The girl shook hands with the diminutive Kelling and immediately led him indoors. Brown presumed that she and the medico were going to where the injured people were lying without delay and, after attaching his mount to the hitching post, he turned to the farmer — who had just seated himself on a nearby windowsill — and said: "About like you put it. No problems with Tompkins."

"He's all right," Whiteman agreed. "Ferguson is unconscious. I don't think he's in any danger, but he sure is hurting more than's good."

"I daresay the doc will give him

laudanum or something."

"They do wonders these days," the farmer acknowledged. "Get a few years on 'em, my boy, and folk won't die at all. Think o' that."

"I'm saving my tears for the undertakers."

"You're an irreverent young varmint, Jack Brown," Whiteman said, whistling up his red dog. "Your pals are in the root shed yonder."

"They're no pals of mine."

"But you're going to join 'em?"

"Reckon."

Whiteman lifted himself from the windowsill and yawned. "Me and the dawg are goin' to do some work."

"The dog mostly, I reckon," Brown commented, giving the animal a pat. "One thing."

"What's that?"

"You know about Clyde Riches?"

"Oriel Beerbohm's told me somethin', yes," the farmer replied. "He's a no-good hellion who needs a hanging to put him right."

"You know all you need to know about Clyde Riches okay," Brown said. "I have half a notion I spotted the sidewinder sneakin' around while me and the doctor were riding in."

"He won't try anything, will he?" Whiteman queried, trying to hide his sudden disquiet. "He's not that crazy is he, Brown?"

"I can't truly believe so," Brown responded. "But it won't do any harm to keep an eye out."

"You folk have brought me trouble I could have done without," Whiteman declared a trifle bitterly. "Why does being a good neighbour always have to hurt? Hell, there's safety in numbers! I'll stick close to the house."

"Sure," Brown said soothingly. "This must be the safest spot for miles."

They parted. Whiteman moved to his left and round the side of the dwelling, while Brown crossed the yard towards the root shed. Coming to the front of the building, he entered by a door that stood ajar, then moved into the gloomy spaces beyond. The atmosphere was not unpleasant — though it smelled of dried earth and decaying vegetable matter — and men, still unknown to Brown in any personal sense, sat around the damp-stained walls, using boxes and piles of sacks for seats. Brown nodded politely to those present, but they took little notice of him; so, shoving a small barrel into place against the wall on his right, he sat down and folded his arms. He decided to rest for a few minutes, then ride out and do a few circuits of the farm. If Clyde Riches were around, he might get a clear glimpse of the man at some point; but he saw no sense in straying too far afield. The prairie was a big place, and the colonel might be anywhere upon it, so it could hardly be of use to deliberately expose himself to danger when he might be needed here.

After a while Brown put his plan into operation. Going to his horse, he mounted up and rode out onto the higher edges of the plain around the farm, jogging a watch that proved as futile as he expected; and, after repeating the pattern of rest and exercise a time or two, he decided to enter the farmhouse kitchen — where he spotted Mrs Whiteman at work — and beg a sandwich; and he was still chewing and studying the tabletop before him, when Oriel Beerbohm entered the room from the upper floor of the house and said: "There you are, Jack."

"Yep," he agreed. "What can I do for you?"

"Will you accompany Doctor Kelling back to the Kansas and Northern construction camp, please?" the blonde asked.

"Sure."

"You can stay over there for the night if you like."

"Kelling will be coming back this way tomorrow morning?"

"First thing."

"Righto."

"You don't mind, Jack?" the girl

inquired. "I feel we ought to show the man this respect, yes?"

"Damn right!" Brown agreed. "How's Mr Ferguson?"

"Comfortable," Orie answered. "He's asleep now. It will take a day or two to get him and the others in a fit state to travel."

Doctor Kelling soon appeared in the kitchen. The little man drank a cup of coffee, while giving Oriel a few instructions for the care of his patient during the dark hours, and then he walked with Brown into the farmyard and they mounted their horses and spurred off the property, the shadows of the evening now smoking into the rich gold of the skyline at their backs. Once more they journeyed without speaking much, and the ride eastwards was as uneventful as that in the opposite direction had been several hours ago.

It was growing dusky by the time they reentered the construction camp. Quintus Tompkins met them outside his tent. Doctor and manager talked awhile, and Tompkins sanctioned Kelling's return to the Whiteman farm at dawn tomorrow. After that he gave Brown the virtual freedom of the construction camp — including the mess and factor's tents if he so wished — and then boss and doctor went their way and Brown was left to do what he pleased with the hours between that time and sunup.

Brown had a beer or two in the factor's tent, while listening to a barrel-organ that was grinding away for the benefit of a dancing monkey, but nothing seemed to please him all that much just then and darkness had not long fallen when he left the factor's canvas domain and went back to his horse. Now he led the animal into the shelter of the oak tree about which part of the camp had been set out. Here he untied and lifted down his bedroll, then picked his spot and unrolled his blankets.

Stretching out in such comfort as he could find, Brown yawned drowsily and relaxed, hands behind his head as he gazed at the stars that patterned the small gaps in the foliage above him and listened to the plaintive chirping of a snow bunting. Yet though sleep was close, it didn't come, and he watched the moon rise and soften the rough lines of the shapes around him with its pale light. He was still awake beyond midnight, and the hours were beginning to seem interminable. He hated nights like these. This kind of sleeplessness damaged a man. Tomorrow he wouldn't be worth a light.

Nor was the camp that still. It was full of men, and he was not the only restless soul around. He heard occasional footsteps, and there were flashes of light too, while the slow panting of a locomotive in which the steam was being kept up was less hypnotic than might have been imagined. Distracted, Brown forced himself to concentrate upon no detail in particular, and it was because of this that he ignored a number of faint rending sounds from the further side of one of the sheds standing on the western perimeter of the camp nearby for longer than he should have done, and it was only when he picked up a faint noise of boots in running retreat that he realized there was cause for suspicion and that he had been indifferent to the point of nonchalance.

Rising from his blankets, Brown reminded himself that he didn't belong here and had every excuse for ignoring the slight disturbance that had gone before; but he found himself walking out from beneath the oak tree nevertheless and approaching the grass beyond, where he halted and peered westwards intently; for out there, under what was largely a clear sky, the moon was casting down light enough to illuminate the prairie for quite a distance.

Brown focused at a spot where a just perceptible change in the heavens caused the shadows to merge and dissolve. Shapes, black but tangible, edged back under the land. Men and horses for sure. Brown had the impression that the mounts were being trotted clear, from the bit, by masters intent on making the least display or noise possible. Were the mounts already burdened? Yes, those fellows over there were almost certainly thieves. His motion involuntary, Brown started after the retiring figures, watching them dodge the moon as they hit leather and spurred at once into a gallop, their speed immediately taking them far beyond any hope that the watcher had of catching them up. Now they were gone, phantoms at the end of a moonbeam that smudged their direction, and the murmur of fading hooves was little louder than the breeze riffling through the grass.

Hesitating then, Brown once again reminded himself that he had no involvement by place or responsibility here, but his wider interest in the men just seen and their doings tonight remained a legitimate one. If robbers had indeed just rifled a building on the edge of the Kansas and Northern's construction camp, they had undoubtedly been men committed to evil ways, and there could not be too many of the like around. In fact Colonel Riches and the survivors of his bunch probably accounted for all; so that in itself was reason enough to give chase and seek a closer look at the miscreants.

Now decided, Brown sprang about and returned to the oak tree under which his blankets were spread. It took him a minute flat to roll up his bed and tie it back behind his saddle. Then he ran his horse out to the grass and mounted up. Aiming the animal's nose, he put spurs to hide and headed for the spot at which he had seen the intruders pass from view into the dark ocean of shadow conjured by the moon. After that he simply rode, travelling by hope and guesswork, and it was several minutes later — and he was offguard in so far as everything outside his main purpose was concerned — when he became aware of numerous riders who were closing in from all sides of him and a man's voice that shouted: "Rein back, mister — or you're dead!"

Brown lay back in his seat, skidding his horse to a standstill, and then he raised his hands above his head. He had recognised the voice that had challenged him, and this was no night to get killed on the failure of others to correctly identify him. Damned if it was! "This is Jack Brown, Mr Foster," he announced as calmly as he could. "You all know about me."

Foster's aquiline features pushed in closer. "It's you all right, Brown. What are you on the gallop for out here? You're supposed to be in another place."

"Don't deny it," Brown answered, feeling it wiser at this point to avoid saying anything that was speculative and to avoid all direct references to his behaviour until he knew what the men from Whiteman's farm were out riding the range for at this hour. "You guys like me? Couldn't you sleep either?"

"We've got new trouble," Foster returned. "It's Orie Beerbohm."

"She's disappeared, son," 'Inky' Whiteman's voice put in from Don Foster's left.

"How disappeared?" Brown demanded sharply.

"We figure she's been abducted," Foster said.

"You aren't sure?" Brown responded, his scowl finding its way into his voice.

"We're sure," Foster snapped. "Her horse is still at its tethering place, and she had told us that she was going for a walk on the farm when the dusk came down. She'd had a day nursing folk, and she needed to stretch her legs."

"This is Colonel Riches's work," Brown stated. "I had half a notion I'd seen him sneaking around much earlier in the day."

"It's him all right," Foster agreed.

"But why? It's hard to see what he can gain."

"Revenge," Foster said. "Act of sheer badness. It's always worse when it's a woman."

"Revenge?" Brown mused. "Why didn't Riches simply kill her and have done with it? He's got to be after something. Can't be me. I don't rate that high." He grunted to himself. "Seems he wanted to draw us all into his orbit, Mr Foster."

"I can't make sense of it either," the other commented. "He can't have anything to gain by doing that. He's asking to wind up dead if he gets caught in the middle of us all. He needs to ride fast and hard — for somewhere like the Hole-in-the-Wall. A hostage, as such, can only be a weight around his neck. At least to begin with; and the start's all he would get."

"He could mean to kill her at some place that has meaning for him," Brown hazarded. "But that wouldn't fit with his character. Colonel Riches is no 'Canada Bill' Jones. He's a man who makes it all count; he never wastes a move. That's why the Yankees feared him so. Anderson, Quantrill, Dingus James; those sons-of-bitches were predictable, gents; but Clyde Riches outthought the bluecoats at every turn. No, I can't really see the colonel simply murdering Orie Beerbohm and then leaving her corpse out any place for us to find."

"You're not much help," Foster said. "But we can't stop searching for her."

"I'd kick up more fuss than all the rest of you put together if we did," Brown informed him. "This seems to me like a night of real fishy goings on."

"What do you mean by that?"

"All a manner of speaking," Brown said. "Tonight I heard sounds back at the railroad camp that I'm sure were caused by breaking and entering."

"A robbery?"

"Uh, huh," Brown grunted, and went

on to provide Foster and the other horsemen who ringed him about with a fairly detailed account of the incident which had been responsible for his riding back in this direction. "I couldn't take my affy on anything that happened back there," he concluded, "except my doings and reading of it; but I've got a feeling there's a connection."

"Why?" Foster asked shortly.

"Two crimes committed at about the same time."

"That's flimsy, Brown!"

"If you've got something better, Mr Foster — ?"

"I haven't, and you know I haven't," Foster retorted, "but what you're offering has little logic to it and no certainty. You've said as much yourself."

"Happen you're right," Brown said curtly. "Maybe I'm offering a recipe for wasting time. So what are we left with but another one for riding round in circles?"

"But what — what exactly do you

have in mind?" Foster spluttered. "I'd go along with anything I had a clear idea about."

"I'm not clear about anything myself yet," Brown reminded. "I've got the glimmerings of an idea, and I'm groping. Really, I suppose, it concerns the colonel and a memory I have."

"A memory of what?"

"Time enough to go into that, Mr Foster," Brown said, "if I come upon any proof I could be right. We can't chew the fat forever."

"Very well," Foster acknowledged reluctantly. "You want to ride back to the construction camp — and us with you?"

"Yes," Brown answered, at his most downright. "I want to find out what exactly — if anything at all — was stolen from there tonight."

"On your head be it then," Foster sighed. "I'm at my wits' end." He raised his voice. "Okay, everybody — let's ride! Brown will lead!"

Brown fetched his horse round and

they set off eastwards, the noise of their progress rumbling through the earth and their flitting shadows cast by the moon towards the low stars of the black north. They rode without let, and the few miles between them and their goal were covered in fifteen minutes. Reining in just short of the railroad camp's western perimeter, Brown dismounted — then asked his companions to remain where they were, for he wished to do all that had to be done without disturbing the entire site — and, as Foster and the other riders clustered at his back, he hurried down into the camp and awakened Quintus Tompkins, who was sleeping on a truckle bed at the back of his office tent and with a lantern suspended above his head. The man was none too pleased at being awakened, and couldn't quite grasp what had happened at first; but, having dipped his head in a bucket of water and heard what Brown had to say three times over, he appeared to grasp that there was a strong suspicion of robbery having occurred in the camp an hour or two ago and went stamping off alone to get his foreman out of bed.

Tompkins rejoined Brown before long, and with him came a dog-eared scrap of a man — who constantly rasped a whiskery chin and listened to everything with a tight jaw and a narrowed eye — and the three of them went to the perimeter sheds where Brown had earlier heard the sounds of stealthy activity and the lanterns that Tompkins and the foreman carried at once revealed that the door to the shed housing the construction crew's explosives had been jemmied open and the contents of the little store place removed. "If that ain't a facer, boss!" the foreman declared. "There's enough dynamite gone to blow up the main street!"

"What will head office say?" Tompkins moaned. "No such thing has ever happened before. We have to keep the stuff at the edge of camp for safety's sake."

"Well, it's sure as hell gone with somebody who aims to do some blasting," the foreman reflected.

"And soon," Brown added, trying to keep a note of triumph out of his voice.

"It's not stuff you keep hanging about," the foreman agreed.

"But who'd want to steal a hundred and fifty pounds of dynamite?" the construction boss demanded, his tones rising to an exasperated wail that belied his bulk.

"I think I know, Mr Tompkins," Brown said. "It concerns matters you needn't worry about. I've friends waiting outside the camp. We'll take care of it."

"Is that all you're going to tell me?" Tompkins bleated. "It's a mess, Brown; and it's my mess. I've got to clear it up."

"You do that," Brown said. "You fret all you want. The theft concerns a missing girl — unless I'm a million miles off the mark — and her welfare is all that matters."

"But — ?"

"Another time," Brown interrupted firmly, turning away. "So long."

Brown hurried back to where he'd left his horse. Remounting, he withdrew from the construction camp and rejoined the men who were waiting for him not far away. Then, ignoring the questions that flew at him, he led Don Foster and the rest back into the prairie, and it was not until they were well clear of the railroad camp — and there could be no question of folk shouting after them and causing further delays — that he said in a loud enough voice for most present to hear: "It's just exactly what I was afraid of. The camp's explosive store had been broken into and a load of dynamite taken. Colonel Riches is planning a mine — of that you may be sure. The best way of killing a lot of men is to catch them in one big bang. You draw them in like wasps to a honey pot. Oriel Beerbohm is the honey pot. Then and wherever we go in to rescue her, there'll be a mine waiting that's planned to blow up and send us all to Glory — Orie included. It's a scheme Clyde Riches has used before. Matter-of-fact, I saw him and his officers use it several times during the war. Never failed!"

"It can only work if we go for the honey pot," Don Foster reminded. "Where will that be? We don't have second sight — do you?"

"No," Brown answered, "but we do have Mr Whiteman."

"What the deuce has he got to do with it?" Foster asked in a mystified voice.

"You can say that again!" the farmer called in rather angrily from amidst the increasingly bunched up riders following Brown and Foster. "I've had me a day, and now I'm having a night — all courtesy of you lot! What's special about me, young Brown?"

"You know these parts," Brown pointed out.

"So what?"

"Can't you think of someplace that girl might be held," Brown inquired, "where Riches could get us all bunched up and then blow us to Kingdom Come? There can't be too many such spots around. I know it sounds a long shot — and maybe you find it hard to swallow — but it sure makes sense to me. The colonel is giving us credit for intelligence, and that's some more of him — when it suits."

"I guess it does fit, if it comes to that," Whiteman suddenly acknowledged.

"You've some idea?" Brown prompted.

"Yeah — sort of," the farmer confessed. "There was once a guy named Thomas Lack who believed he'd found a ridge o' silver not fifteen miles northwest of here. He built him a nice big cabin, down in a hollow, tucked under the side of that rim. The cabin is still there, but its builder ain't. The ridge didn't yield enough silver to keep Lack in dry goods. I hope he's doin' better in hell."

"You think that's where we should

ride?" Brown asked.

"You wanted me to make a guess," the farmer returned, "and that's my best one. There ain't what you might call a whole crop of choices. Not in this g'damned emptiness, there ain't. That'd be part of your colonel too, maybe?"

"He's quick as you like," Brown agreed. "Mr Foster?"

"I leave it to you," Foster replied.

"Show us the way then, 'Inky'!" Brown called to the farmer.

"I said northwest," Whiteman reminded. "You know where that is as well as I do!"

Brown raised a hand and shifted the party's heading.

11

The night was fast getting away, and the country lay black and seemingly without shape where the moon had never pressed a passing foot. Presently the wind got up. It blew cold, and the new grass hissed audibly under its sweeping pressure. Brown's visual impressions were few, but his discomfort was great, for he still lacked underwear and his outer garments were not thick enough to save him from shivering.

Still sure of nothing, his mood was low, and he had the feeling that he was on a ride without end. The plains could even be swallowing him and his companions alive. He wished the night over and the world a year on. There was a crisis to come and he would prefer it finished with. He had few doubts that he and the men with whom he was riding would emerge the winners from whatever test they had to undergo, and it was not the fact of death so much as who would have to die that most troubled him. If Riches died, it was probable that Oriel Beerbohm would have to do the same. When prompting a showdown, most men could be relied upon to bungle something, but the colonel could be trusted to get the killing right every time. Riches loomed in Brown's imagination just then like the shape of Doom itself; and that was foolish; because his common sense told him that the colonel was only a man who had been too long feared due to the craven attitude which others had taken towards him.

More time went by, and the setting moon took the wind down with it. A dead calm heralded the coming of the dawn. Grey light pushed back the receding darkness, and the land began to take shape before the still advancing horsemen. Then, looking up,

Brown had the impression of a rocky crest crossing the insubstantial scene ahead. "There's the rim I was tellin' you about," Whiteman said, pointing. "That fellow Lack blew and chopped it about somethin' wicked. There's a hollow below it and to our left. The cabin stands down there."

"I think we should hold back until it's completely light," Don Foster said. "We're riding up with the dawn at our backs."

"We're not yet visible against the ground," Brown responded. "Nor do we have any guarantee there's anybody up there looking down. Let's get in close while we've got the chance. If there is anybody watching, they'll see us all the better later on. We don't want to be seen at all for now."

Foster grunted, but offered no counter word. The riders kept on approaching the ridge, and soon they were within a quarter of a mile of their goal. Screwing round in his saddle, he saw the pale glow of first light rising and deepening at their backs. The dayspring was now becoming a threat, but he was still of no mind to slow up; so, to further eliminate the risk of their being spotted — or even becoming targets — he suggested that everybody dismount and go forward now on foot; but, before Brown got a reaction of any kind, a glow rose from beneath the ground off their left shoulders and turned red, tongues of fire leaping amidst it and clouds of sooty smoke boiling up.

"It's the cabin!" Whiteman bawled. "Somebody's put it to the torch! Why would anybody do that?"

Brown clapped his spurs into hide, and his horse bounded forward, stretching and tucking in angry surprise, and its rider had not covered a further three hundred yards, when the answer to Whiteman's last question became plain, for a woman could be heard shrieking for help down in the blaze.

"That's Oriel Beerbohm!" Foster shouted. "They're burning her alive!"

The words seemed to throw a kind

215

of panic into the horsemen. Now they made for the fire at a pace that had no hint of caution left in it. They galloped unchecked into the rising firelight, and then the ground dropped abruptly into a hole before them, forcing the kind of stop which brought the horses down on their tails. The men spilled out of leather; then, led by Brown, they raced to the top of a steep path on their right and sprang downwards, skidding and scuffing on the surfaces below, Brown at the same time catching his first glimpse of a large cabin which stood amidst the fierce oil blaze that was already starting to consume it.

Brown arrived on the floor of the low. Flinging his head back, he gasped in the heat and stink present, seeing above him, as he coughed a huge overhang jutting from the hillside adjacent. This seemed to be holding the smoke-filled air down, and he dodged left to avoid it, flinging himself at the door in the front of the log-house and ignoring his fear that a vast explosion might send him and the building sky-high at any moment. He struck the door with his left shoulder, all his weight and strength going into the collision, and the lock shattered out of the woodwork and everything went whirling inwards on shrilling hinges.

Before him now Brown saw a relatively smoke-free hall that crossed the middle of the dwelling. Catching a foot on a broken floorboard, he blundered indoors; then, swearing as he recovered himself, he began looking around him with eyes that watered and stung. He made out a single door in each of the walls on either hand, and Orie Beerbohm's cries came to him from behind that on his left. Lunging at the door, he forced it open without much difficulty and entered a bare, dirt-hung room that seemed full of garish, pulsing light. He saw the girl opposite. She was bound hand and foot, and sitting in the fireplace with her legs drawn up. Raw flesh at her wrists and ankles showed how frantically she had already fought her bonds, and he signalled for her to lie still as he crouched to free her — but he had lately perceived that something here didn't entirely add up; for, had the desire been to simply incinerate the girl, a gag would have been tied into her mouth and her silence ensured while she died. As it was, not only had she been left free to shout for help but the fire itself had clearly been lighted at a moment timed to give Brown and his companions a short space in which to attempt the shrieking girl's rescue. One way or another, this was the honey pot and the flies had been drawn in about it — for all the riders who had come to this place were now down in the hollow with Brown — and there could be no question but that the swat was to be a total one and soon. As expected, it could only be the dynamite — blasting from somewhere other than the foundations of the cabin — and Brown's mind went at once to the overhang that lowered towards this building from the hillside adjacent. If an explosion brought that down, this cabin would be instantly flattened and buried under hundreds of tons of rock and earth. The untying of bonds was not to be contemplated in the circumstances, and Brown snatched Orie Beerbohm up into his arms without more ado, yelling to the men who had now packed into the room at his back: "Get out of here fast! Riches is going to blast down that mass of stone which overhangs the roof on top of us!"

He turned to meet faces that were shocked and drained, surging at the men with the blonde held tightly to his chest. Then those about the door jostled round and forced their way back into the hall outside, shouting and clawing as they headed for the open, and Brown moved after them, blocked off from the cabin's front door for what seemed like an eternity. Then his path began to clear, and he forged ahead, steering the girl's frame as best he could and, coughing and choking and half blinded, he emerged from the log-house and squinted upwards, knowing full well that he could never climb the steep path beyond him burdened as he was and with others slipping and elbowing around him.

A pulse in his brain gave an instinctive warning that the seconds were running out. For a split instant he paused, peering up and round, and he saw, as plainly as could be, the powder-based sparks of several fuses spitting out of the collar of blackness which encircled the base of the overhang. He had got it exactly right — curse his own exaggerated perceptions! — but, with all his quickness to see and act, was trapped as surely as if he had been the worst dimwit present.

There had got to be a way out of this. Some form of salvation always surfaced. His muscles were tired, his lungs were choked, and he simply wasn't thinking clearly. Then it occurred to him that a man had lived down here and that there had to be space around the building — and possibly even a path out of the hollow at this lower level — so he staggered off blindly to his right and beyond the cabin's southern end, the narrow spit of open ground thrusting between high jaws of grass and revealing a prospect of smoky safety beyond.

Reeling and lurching, Brown entered the back of the jaws and there his strength gave out. Dropping the girl, he fell on top of her, spreading his body to provide her with the maximum protection, and he was lying thus when a mighty flash split the lingering shadows of this early hour and a vast shudder passed through the land, while the sweeping blast of a tremendous bang snatched the air away from his nostrils and deafened him. He lay there in a momentary vacuum, and debris rained down upon him, but none of it large enough to cause him real harm. His senses rocking, he suddenly felt the struggling of Orie's limbs beneath his own and her panic forced him to roll aside and lie there prone, the front of his body pumping painfully as his strength gradually returned and his wits cleared. It was done, by God — they had come through!

Yet he realized dully that the danger was not over. His enhanced perceptions were with him again. Every nerve in his body was responding to the slow and watchful movements of a man approaching across the grass before him. Brown raised his chin and peered to the front, noting that the oncoming figure had already entered his field of foreshortened perspectives. The question of identity was also distorted and momentarily odd, but the man yonder was undoubtedly Clyde Riches. The colonel, watching from somewhere high, would have had the over-all view of what had just occurred and seen him escape the fire and pursuing explosion with Oriel Beerbohm in his arms. The outcome of events must have been a sickening disappointment to Clyde Riches — and he must also have the deepest of renewed worries concerning his future — but he had obviously come down to be revenged upon the one man who had, so much more than all the others, been responsible for thwarting his schemes at every turn. Brown could understand how the other felt and there was no fear in him as he considered this final accounting.

They must fight. Shoving himself to his feet, Brown touched his holster — making sure that his gun was in place — and then he brushed himself off and faced his enemy squarely. "Good morning, Colonel," he greeted, his hands dropping loosely to his sides. "Your move, sir."

"Thank you, Brown," the other acknowledged, inclining his head in a mock bow. "That you should challenge me."

"We're both men."

"I'm going to kill you, Brown."

"No, sir. You're going to try."

They went for their pistols. Riches made the faster draw, but fired and missed. Brown triggered a split second later, his aim the steadier one, and the colonel staggered as lead burned into his vitals. Yet he fetched up again and, though his face was twisted by an unspeakable agony, tried to improve on his first effort, but he succeeded only in lifting the dirt at his opponent's feet. Brown gazed steadily at Riches then, raising his aim, put a bullet through the colonel's brain. Riches collapsed, instantly unstrung, and he lay motionless. Brown didn't even bother to walk over and give him a kick. The colonel would only wake up again in hell.

Holstering his gun, Brown walked to where Orie Beerbohm lay among the tussocks, still tied at her hands and feet. Kneeling, he undid the bindings and then sat her up, grinning wickedly as he gazed into her eyes. "Orie," he said, "you owe me."

"Yes," she agreed, "and you're rat enough to collect."

"Seems you have me pegged," he

agreed complacently. "I'm going home with you, when you go, and I'm going to see my little girl."

"That's emotional blackmail," Orie complained, "and I won't have it."

"Gotta say something, haven't you?"

"Jack, if that little mite sees you, you'll never get away again," the blonde warned. "You're two of a kind."

"That's what I'm counting on," he confessed.

"You're impossible!" the girl declared, turning her face to heaven. "How am I going to keep the two of you in order?"

"Oh, I daresay you'll manage," Brown said comfortably, bending and kissing her on the lips.

THE END

TOP HAND
Wade Everett

The Broken T was big. But no ranch is big enough to let a man hide from himself.

GUN WOLVES OF LOBO BASIN
Lee Floren

The Feud was a blood debt. When Smoke Talbot found the outlaws who gunned down his folks he aimed to nail their hide to the barn door.

SHOTGUN SHARKEY
Marshall Grover

The westbound coach carrying the indomitable Larry and Stretch headed for a shooting showdown.

FIGHTING RAMROD
Charles N. Heckelmann

Most men would have cut their losses, but Frazer counted the bullets in his guns and said he'd soak the range in blood before he'd give up another inch of what was his.

LONE GUN
Eric Allen

Smoke Blackbird had been away too long. The Lequires had seized the Blackbird farm, forcing the Indians and settlers off, and no one seemed willing to fight! He had to fight alone.

THE THIRD RIDER
Barry Cord

Mel Rawlins wasn't going to let anything stand in his way. His father was murdered, his two brothers gone. Now Mel rode for vengeance.

ARIZONA DRIFTERS
W. C. Tuttle

When drifting Dutton and Lonnie Steelman decide to become partners they find that they have a common enemy in the formidable Thurston brothers.

TOMBSTONE
Matt Braun

Wells Fargo paid Luke Starbuck to outgun the silver-thieving stagecoach gang at Tombstone. Before long Luke can see the only thing bearing fruit in this eldorado will be the gallows tree.

HIGH BORDER RIDERS
Lee Floren

Buckshot McKee and Tortilla Joe cut the trail of a border tough who was running Mexican beef into Texas. They stopped the smuggler in his tracks.

BRETT RANDALL, GAMBLER
E. B. Mann

Larry Day had the choice of running away from the law or of assuming a dead man's place. No matter what he decided he was bound to end up dead.

THE GUNSHARP
William R. Cox

The Eggerleys weren't very smart. They trained their sights on Will Carney and Arizona's biggest blood bath began.

THE DEPUTY OF SAN RIANO
Lawrence A. Keating and
Al. P. Nelson

When a man fell dead from his horse, Ed Grant was spotted riding away from the scene. The deputy sheriff rode out after him and came up against everything from gunfire to dynamite.

FARGO: MASSACRE RIVER
John Benteen

The ambushers up ahead had now blocked the road. Fargo's convoy was a jumble, a perfect target for the insurgents' weapons!

SUNDANCE: DEATH IN THE LAVA
John Benteen

The Modoc's captured the wagon train and its cargo of gold. But now the halfbreed they called Sundance was going after it . . .

HARSH RECKONING
Phil Ketchum

Five years of keeping himself alive in a brutal prison had made Brand tough and careless about who he gunned down . . .

FARGO: PANAMA GOLD
John Benteen

With foreign money behind him, Buckner was going to destroy the Panama Canal before it could be completed. Fargo's job was to stop Buckner.

FARGO:
THE SHARPSHOOTERS
John Benteen

The Canfield clan, thirty strong were raising hell in Texas. Fargo was tough enough to hold his own against the whole clan.

PISTOL LAW
Paul Evan Lehman

Lance Jones came back to Mustang for just one thing — revenge! Revenge on the people who had him thrown in jail.

HELL RIDERS
Steve Mensing

Wade Walker's kid brother, Duane, was locked up in the Silver City jail facing a rope at dawn. Wade was a ruthless outlaw, but he was smart, and he had vowed to have his brother out of jail before morning!

DESERT OF THE DAMNED
Nelson Nye

The law was after him for the murder of a marshal — a murder he didn't commit. Breen was after him for revenge — and Breen wouldn't stop at anything . . . blackmail, a frameup . . . or murder.

DAY OF THE COMANCHEROS
Steven C. Lawrence

Their very name struck terror into men's hearts — the Comancheros, a savage army of cutthroats who swept across Texas, leaving behind a bloodstained trail of robbery and murder.

SUNDANCE: SILENT ENEMY
John Benteen

A lone crazed Cheyenne was on a personal war path. They needed to pit one man against one crazed Indian. That man was Sundance.

LASSITER
Jack Slade

Lassiter wasn't the kind of man to listen to reason. Cross him once and he'll hold a grudge for years to come — if he let you live that long.

LAST STAGE TO GOMORRAH
Barry Cord

Jeff Carter, tough ex-riverboat gambler, now had himself a horse ranch that kept him free from gunfights and card games. Until Sturvesant of Wells Fargo showed up.

McALLISTER
ON THE
COMANCHE CROSSING
Matt Chisholm

The Comanche, McAllister owes them a life — and the trail is soaked with the blood of the men who had tried to outrun them before.

QUICK-TRIGGER COUNTRY
Clem Colt

Turkey Red hooked up with Curly Bill Graham's outlaw crew. But wholesale murder was out of Turk's line, so when range war flared he bucked the whole border gang alone . . .

CAMPAIGNING
Jim Miller

Ambushed on the Santa Fe trail, Sean Callahan is saved by two Indian strangers. But there'll be more lead and arrows flying before the band join Kit Carson against the Comanches.